L.L. ABBOTT
ECHOES
OF GUILT
A
Lake
Pines
Mystery

WELCOME TO LAKE PINES

Where the scenery is beautiful, but the secrets are deadly.

A fictional small town in Northwestern Ontario that's home to both year-round residents and summer cottagers. Hidden secrets, private lives, and tension lay the groundwork for treacherous crimes. But there are more than secrets buried in this small town.

LAKE PINES MURDER MYSTERY SERIES

Murder at First Light

Death at Deception Bay

Murder of Crows

The Dead of Winter

The Night is Darkest

Conspiracy of Blood

Deadly Past

Echoes of Guilt

Dead in the Water

A Dark, Dark Truth

Last to Die

ECHOES OF GUILT

A gripping, suspenseful mystery

L.L. Abbott

Cover designed by Warren Design

L.L. Abbott
www.LLAbbott.com

Hemlock & Ash

Large Print Paperback ISBN 1-989325-79-7

For people who have come before us.
For without them we would not be here,
and our guide for where we should go would be unclear.

"Very few of us are what we seem."

- Agatha Christie

ECHOES OF GUILT

CHAPTER 1

Sections of yellow tape, bowed and bent between crooked poles, wrestled with the wind. Other than the noise caused by the flapping with each gust, the whistling gale dulled every sound across the field. Murmurs between two officers who intentionally kept their voices hushed were inaudible from where Kerry stood, and she could only speculate as to what they were talking about. Eventually, the awkwardness of the moment quieted their conversation and they stepped away from each other.

Simon directed the five officers who arrived from the station, scattering them across the meadow. Some were tasked with blocking access to the field, while others repositioned the poles and yellow tape when it became apparent that more space would be necessary.

The ends of Kerry's hair whipped around her face, each strand stabbing at the base of her jaw. She tried to ignore the fragrant breeze combined with the warmth rising on the back of her neck, not because it was unpleasant, but because it seemed misplaced.

Lake Pines was emerging from an extended winter, one that had stretched into April and where temperatures dipped below the normal average.

In fact, the warmth was a welcome sensation when she rushed out the front door that morning. But as Kerry stood a hundred feet away from where the forensic team was working, she wondered if a cold steely gray sky would be more in keeping with the mood that was rapidly collapsing over everyone at the crime scene.

No one spoke. Everyone averted their eyes from one another as they remained transfixed around the crime scene. They were inescapably mesmerized by what was happening in the field, just beyond the perimeter of the flapping yellow tape.

Kerry remained motionless as the forensic team had reached another body.

Another grave.

Another stabbing question.

Her job as the coroner, required her attendance at the site, as it did for every crime scene in Lake Pines. However, when she received the call six hours earlier, it was because a hiker and his dog came across a partially buried body. That body arrived at her lab several hours ago. It was what the police had found shortly after the first body was removed from the ground that prompted her return to the field.

It was a haunting clue of a different crime. This one was much older than the one that the police were called about earlier in the day and Kerry instinctively knew it would generate more questions once the exhumation was complete.

They were standing at Belvedere Field. Although there wasn't an official town sign posted at the edge of the property, the vacant lot next to the forest had been called that for as long as anyone could remember.

Twisted trails in the dense forest paths opened onto a clearing where rough-hewn benches were perched along the shoreline, welcoming visitors to sit and enjoy the view at the scenic bend in the river. It was a place of peaceful relaxation.

Over the last few years, the forest became a popular area where dog owners could run with their pets. Unencumbered by leashes or rules as they challenged themselves over rocky mounts, steep gullies, and fallen trees. Kerry had ventured through these same trails several times on a hike or a run. Sometimes she was alone but most times it was Raven's need for exercise that drew her to these trails. However, his propensity to chase squirrels eventually cautioned her against off-lease runs.

Now, looking down at the land which was dotted with unearthed patches of ground, it was difficult to imagine the happier moments spent on the field. Kerry tried to conjure up memories of sunny picnics and impromptu soccer games but the harshness of the moment pushed them away. Instead, she was focused on the small rectangles of grass that were peeled back revealing a sinister clue of a buried crime.

Kerry wondered how long the body had remained concealed, literally under everyone's feet. She'd have to wait until she examined the remains in her lab before she drew any conclusion of what it was that lay underneath the most recent thaw. The remains were definitely human, but the reason for their placement in the public park would be the question at the forefront of everyone's mind.

More than one crime cast a shadow over the field. Neither of the crimes had occurred at the same time nor by the same perpetrator, but the implications of what lay beneath the windswept land could no longer be ignored.

A gust pushed against Kerry's back, and the trees in the forest boughed to the chaotic pattern of the wind, tipping their tops toward the unearthed graves below. She pulled her shoulders close to her neck and folded her arms across the front of her body. The determined course of the wind cascaded over the field, flattening the long grass in waves that came with each shift in direction. Its power was only interrupted by the disturbed areas of ground where the first body, and then subsequent remains, had been found. The motion of the grass mirrored that of the water just beyond the edge of the property at the bottom of the hill. Ominously reminding everyone standing on that field that nature was still in control. With each gust, Mother Nature screamed as if to say she was a witness to a crime that no one had discovered until today.

There were indications of an older crime that was concealed below the most recent grave. Clues and fragments that would have gone unnoticed, had it not been for the discovery of the most recent murder victim.

Lake Pines' latest killer had buried the body in haste, leaving a thin surface of soil defenseless against the harsh lake wind, and caused the accidental discovery of the victim. The hiker was shocked when he came upon his dog tugging at the frayed sleeve protruding from the ground, and he pulled the Border Collie away before any damage had been caused to the victim's arm. As he clipped his dog's leash to its collar and pulled him to the top of the hill, he phoned the police and waited, averting his eyes away from the protruding arm. Simon arrived with another officer and after recording the man's statement, allowed the shaken hiker to return home while he called Kerry and the forensic team.

No one predicted that the horrific scene that was discovered early in the morning would be made worse by the end of the day. But it had.

Simon came toward Kerry, ducking under the flimsy stretch of yellow tape, and stood beside her.

"Josh is on his way with some tents," Simon glanced toward the sky. He was growing concerned about the rapid shift in the weather and the approaching rain clouds. "I think a storm is blowing in and I want to get the area covered before we go any further."

"Any idea what we're dealing with here?" Kerry pointed to the unearthed ground.

Simon shook his head, "At first thought, I'd say that the killer rushed to bury a body and maybe didn't realize how often this field is used. Even at this time of year."

"Can you tell if there's something else buried with the older remains that can help us identify the body?"

"It's too soon to tell, but I left a message for Peter. I'm going to call in a favor."

"Why would you call the Superintendent of the Provincial Police department?" Kerry asked. "I know he once ran the Lake Pines Police Department, but how can he help here? We're not even sure what we're dealing with."

"The province has a ground-penetrating radar machine and I'm going to see if he can have it delivered. We'll be able to scan the area and determine exactly where we should dig. It could save us several hours of aimless digging."

"*A* machine? There's only *one*?" Kerry asked, holding up her index finger.

"Yeah, that's why I need the favor. I called just before you arrived and I was told it wasn't available until next week."

A rumble rolled above, diverting their eyes away from the field and toward the sky. As Kerry pulled her jacket closed, a heavy dampness and the earthy scent of impending rain chilled the air, replacing the warm breeze that started the day.

An officer waved in their direction and Simon returned to the field where three officers were kneeling on the ground. Kerry remained at the top of the hill, her focus rapidly shifting toward the west. As the month straddled the seasons, the weather changed quickly, often shifting from a comfortable warmth to a tense chill in a matter of a few hours.

Storm clouds replaced the blue sky that had initially stretched awkwardly over the field and had seemed a traitor to the dire mood that was spreading from one person to the next.

Kerry turned around and walked briskly to her car. There was a body waiting in her lab, and her duty to the first victim that was unearthed earlier in the day hijacked her interest in what was laying in the ground in Belvedere Field.

The dark shadows from the clouds that rolled over the forest, heralded a foreboding sense of the unanswered questions that loomed ahead. Having borne the weight of time, the older set of remains would be subjected to the harshness of the elements, making the determination of who the victim was, or what ended their life, more difficult. But not impossible.

Her first thought was that the approaching storm was more welcome in the space where bodies had been concealed in Lake Pines.

Her second thought was, that up until today, the secrets that lay hidden deep inside the graves were known only to the murderer, or murderers, who placed them there.

CHAPTER 2

A thin deep gash stretched across the victim's neck, extending three-quarters of the way around his throat. Even with the traces of dirt and mud that had accumulated from the shallow grave, it was obvious that the wound had been wiped clean before the victim had been buried.

No scratches or jagged movements marked the victim's neck or the perfectly straight line that severed his two carotid arteries. The wound rested just below the angle of the victim's jaw and was flawlessly aligned with each of his ears.

Almost as if it had been drawn with an artist's pen over his skin.

It was a perfect slice and because of its placement over the vocal cords, it was a wound that would ensure a silent death. The pain would have come in a flash, and the victim would have been aware of what was happening. Even though he wouldn't have been able to survive the loss of blood or been able to elicit a scream, there should have been an instinctive reaction to fight back. Kerry ran a gloved finger along the edge of the wound, gently feeling the surface of the victim's skin and the precision was unsettling.

The extended cut should have revealed some sign of a struggle.

Some resistance.

Instead, the deep gash suggested the use of a large sharp blade on an unconscious victim.

The absence of bloodstains on the victim's clothing also struck Kerry as odd. Murder scenes were never easy to take in, even with the wealth of experience Kerry brought to each case, she always prepared herself for the shock that would inevitably come. The dull waxy flesh, vacant eyes, and blood-soaked clothes were gruesome clues that a person's life had ended violently. But they were clues, nonetheless.

However, Kerry was looking down at a body that seemed to have been prepared for death in the same manner that it appeared to have been prepared for burial.

Initially, Kerry had thought the murder may have been the result of an act of passion. Most of the signs were there. A swift attack, a frantic killer, and a hurried burial.

Now she had to consider a more frightening thought. What if the murderer intended for the body to be found in Belvedere Field and maybe the lack of crime scene evidence on the body was a chilling invitation? Could the killer be taunting the intelligence of those investigating the crime?

At first, Kerry thought the location of the body in the open field seemed like an odd choice for a killer looking to quickly dispose of a body. But the extra cold winter kept many people indoors and the open field may have easily been mistaken for an unused plot of land. It may have been thought to be far enough away from the town and the residents where the murderer could conceal their identity along with the body.

It was even possible that the victim and murderer weren't from Lake Pines. With the increase in cross-country car trips, more strangers traveled through the town in recent years, adding another layer of probability to the identity of the victim. Whether it was a tourist, traveler, or resident, Kerry still needed to find a clue that would help identify the cause of death and hopefully give the victim a name.

Each piece of the victim's clothing was placed on the adjacent table as Kerry examined them for clues. In addition to the absence of a wallet or any identifiable jewelry, the victim wore a pair of faded jeans, a plain navy cotton shirt, and a brown jacket that was stylishly frayed at the collar and sleeves. Each item was non-descript and the person wearing them would easily blend into a crowd. There was nothing in any of the victim's pockets. No wallet, keys, or credit cards. Kerry would have to rely on her autopsy examination, dental records, fingerprints, and photo images to identify the man on her examination table.

The little information she did possess was that the victim was male, close to thirty years of age, and had been dead less than forty-eight hours. His short sandy brown hair was freshly cut and angled at the base of his neck, tapering to a fade. He had blue eyes and fair skin that was free of tattoos or scars, and there were no signs of bruising anywhere on his body.

Luckily the dog had only managed to grab hold of the victim's sleeve, leaving the man's hand unmarked. If Kerry was going to establish who had killed the victim, she needed to determine where he had been. Traces of particles that the victim may have picked up during a struggle with the killer was her main focus.

Kerry swabbed the victim's blackened tongue and took samples of the fine film coating the inside of his mouth. She drew some blood and tissue samples, narrowing her scan to focus on traces of poison or barbiturates. While she awaited the test results, Kerry swabbed the surface of the victim's skin, mouth and then clipped samples of his hair and nails.

She worked in a trance, moving from one process to the next, and soon her mind drifted to the memory of her friend. Wayne had been dead for less than a year and Kerry was still having difficulty coming to terms with his absence, both on the job and in her personal life.

He bridged the gap between her and some residents of Lake Pines who were initially uneasy at accepting an outsider as part of the community. There was an instinct from some senior residents to distrust and be leery of people who moved to Lake Pines. Especially if it was someone with no family connections in the area.

Kerry was an unknown commodity when she replaced Doctor Crampton as the town's coroner. Older residents voiced concerns about her inexperience when they protested her appointment to the job. But in the end, Peter held firm to his opinion that she be hired as the town's coroner and Wayne continued to build trust between Kerry and members of the community.

Even though Lake Pines was now her home, she still longed for the connection Wayne bridged to the town and its people.

Kerry was happy that Wayne's brother Josh and his husband decided to move to Lake Pines. Josh's work in the police department was the connection that Simon needed to Wayne, and Kerry's instant friendship and connection to him and Thomas was the link she needed. But Kerry knew it would take patience and time before her memories would elicit a smile as opposed to tears.

The computer's timer signaled the completion of the tests and the results tumbled from the printer below the counter. Kerry blinked away the dampness rising in her eyes, refocusing on the information she had gathered on the unknown victim.

Skin swabs confirmed the presence of chlorhexidine digluconate and isopropyl alcohol which were compounds found in antibacterial washes. But what were the strong disinfectants doing on the victim's skin?

Her eyes drifted to the second sheet and she saw that not only were the medical-grade antiseptic compounds registering on the surface of the victim's skin, but they were also present on his hair and inside his mouth. The final results showed traces of thiopental in the victim's blood, confirming Kerry's suspicion that the victim was unconscious when his throat was slashed.

The crime was frightful enough, but the idea that the killer took such elaborate steps to conceal all traces of evidence was terrifying. As with any murder, Kerry always considered motive and opportunity, now she was thrust into a dangerous mind that was responsible for a premeditated killing.

She only had a few things to finish before she could complete the report and file a statement of the cause of death. Kerry reached for her blade and just before she opened the chest cavity she lifted the victim's hand.

Under the magnifying lens, Kerry noticed a small black dot that she missed during her initial visual inspection. She dragged the thin metal blade under the nail and placed the particle on a piece of glass. She immediately recognized what was lodged under the victim's nail, but what Kerry didn't understand was why the only foreign element on the victim's body was one small seed.

When she had completed the final steps of the examination, Kerry took several photographs along with fingerprints and dental imprints before she called Simon with a preliminary report.

"I'm sending you a photo of our victim. I believe he was killed between thirty-six and forty-eight hours ago," Kerry said. As she spoke, she typed Simon's email address into her computer and sent the image files to him. "Hopefully that timeline will give you an estimate of where to track his movements. I'm also sending you the scans of his fingerprints and I've already uploaded the dental imprints into the system."

"I'll get Sally to distribute the image to the officers and then I'll get Jamie to run the image and prints through our database and see if we get any hits," Simon said.

"How's Jamie handling the leadership role in the tech department?" Kerry knew that moving Jamie from a support position into the head of the department was a huge leap to ask any employee to make, especially someone so young.

However, Myra Dean's demotion was warranted after she was found tampering with evidence from a criminal investigation.

"He's been great," Simon said. "He and Myra don't seem to have any problem with the switch in their positions."

"That's good to hear. Is there any news from Peter on when the ground-penetrating radar machine will arrive?"

"It's being delivered tomorrow. We'll start scanning as soon as it's light enough for the technician to see the field."

Kerry was eager to know more about the second set of remains in the field and stopped short of inviting herself along to watch the scan.

"Guess what else I learned?" Simon asked and then answered without waiting for Kerry's response. "When I entered the information for the police report, the computer system didn't recognize the name of the park. There is no Belvedere Field registered in any of the town property records. When I did a property search with the geographical coordinates for the field, that parcel of land came back as being privately owned."

"I always thought that meadow was owned by the town of Lake Pines and was part of the forest property."

"Everyone I asked thought it was a public park as well," Simon said. "The only information I could get is that the property is registered to a numbered company. I'll let you know what I find out, but right now I have to go, Josh is waiting for me in the next room. The hiker who found the body is here and we're going to get a full statement from him. I'm hoping he can remember seeing someone else in the area."

Kerry ended the call and then returned to the examination room just as thunder rumbled above in the darkening sky, reverberating through her empty lab. She glanced down at the body, wishing she had a name for the victim in front of her, but all she could envision were his dull vacant eyes screaming for the answers to his murder that she still didn't know enough about.

CHAPTER 3

Rain pounded against the small window in the interview room where Gary Fredricks was waiting – more relaxed and less shaken than he was at Belvedere Field that morning. After speaking with Simon at the site where the body was found, he brought his dog home and then promised to come into the station and give a formal statement. Josh was writing Gary's name and phone number on a witness statement sheet when Simon walked into the room.

Gary Fredricks' height made it difficult for him to find a comfortable position in the plastic chair and the heft of his upper body leaned forward on the table. Simon didn't personally know Gary Fredricks, however, he did recognize his face from frequent, albeit peaceful, environmental protests that took place every summer. He was a member of a small group that promoted the ecological integrity of Lake of the Woods and its watershed by spreading information on water stewardship and raising funds. An oval green and blue lapel pin boasted that Gary Fredricks was a ten-year veteran of the cause, and as far as Simon knew, this was the first time he was inside the police station.

Simon stretched out his hand, "Thank you for coming in Mr. Fredricks."

“Please, call me Gary,” the man smiled and held out his hand. His clasp was simple and strong. “This young officer told me you still don’t know who the victim is.”

“No, we don’t,” Simon pulled out a chair and sat beside Josh. “We’re trying to put a picture together of the man’s movements in the area. It’ll help us narrow down our search.”

Gary folded his fingers together, rested his hands on the table, and smiled, “Whatever I can do to help.”

Simon placed the photograph that Kerry emailed to him on the table and turned it around so Gary could see it clearly.

“This is the man who was buried in the field. Do you recognize him?” Simon asked.

Gary picked up the paper, intrigued that it contained an image of the man who was buried in the ground earlier that day. He shook his head, “No, he doesn’t look familiar at all.”

“How often do you hike through that forest?” Josh asked.

“I try and get Scotch there at least three times a week.”

“Scotch? That’s your dog?” Josh asked.

“Yeah,” Gary laughed. “It was my kid’s idea to name him that because of the color of his fur.”

Josh smiled and wrote down the information on the page, “What days were you there this week?”

Gary rolled his eyes toward the ceiling, mentally flipping through the calendar in his mind, “Thursday, Friday, and then today.”

With a three-day window between Gary's last two visits, it wasn't likely he had seen anything of use.

"Did you happen to see anyone else on the trails today?" Simon asked. "I'm assuming there are regular hikers and runners that use those trails."

"Sure," a relaxed grin rested on Gary's face as he spoke. "As soon as the weather improves, lots of people start to hit the trails, especially after the extra-long cold winter we've just had. There were lots of people out for walks and runs, I'm surprised no one else's dog sniffed out the body."

"Can you give me names of any of the people you saw in the forest?" Josh was poised with his pen ready to write the names of other people he could contact.

“Well, probably only a few,” Gary said, tilting his head sideways. “I see a lot of the same people, but I only know them well enough to say hello, I don’t know their names.”

“Why don’t you give me the names of the people you do know?”

Gary gave Josh the names and addresses of the three people he remembered seeing on the trails that morning. Josh closed the file and rested his pen on the desk.

“That’s it?” Gary asked, surprised at the brevity of the questions.

“You gave us a good statement of what happened on your hike this morning, so outside of that, we’ll just contact these other people and find out if they remember seeing anything suspicious over the last few days.”

“Alright then,” Gary pushed back his chair, stood, and stretched his arm across the table. First toward Simon and then Josh. “You’re new here, aren’t you?” he asked Josh. “I recognize most of the officers and I don’t think I’ve seen you before today.”

Josh smiled, “Sort of. I grew up in Lake Pines, but I’d been living in Toronto for more than a decade.”

“What brought you back to Lake Pines?” Gary smiled and rested his hands on his hips. “That’s quite a change to move from the big city to a small town.”

“My brother was an officer at this station, and after he died, Simon convinced me to take over the vacant position. Eventually, I agreed, and then my husband and I decided to make the move and settle in Lake Pines permanently."

The edges of Gary's smile leveled, and his relaxed arms shifted awkwardly until he finally folded them against his chest, "Husband?"

Josh was prepared for the odd head turn and impolite response, but in all honesty, it was becoming tiresome. "Yes, and our daughter. We've been here for almost nine months."

Gary fidgeted in his stance and then made a motion to look at his watch, "I better get going. It's almost time to feed Scotch." He pulled his jacket off the back of the chair and moved toward the door.

"Thanks for coming in Mr. Fredricks, I'll let you know if we need any more information." Simon held open the door as Gary walked out and shoved it closed, hoping he noticed that Simon dropped his friendly demeanor.

Simon turned toward Josh, "Sorry about that Josh."

Josh shook his head, "Honestly, I've learned to not care about what most people think. My first few months as a recruit in the police force were much harder."

"And Thomas?" Simon asked.

"He's finding the adjustment to small-town life a little more difficult. He loved the crowds and busy downtown lifestyle but he's committed to giving it a fair chance."

"How's Thomas' new construction project coming along?"

When Thomas agreed to move to Lake Pines, he saw it as an opportunity to work on a project he had been dreaming about for years. His plan for an eco-friendly residential complex had suited the surrounding beauty of the lake region but his ultimate plan was to franchise the idea across the country.

"It took him a while to find the right location to build, and then he had to secure the funding for the project," Josh said. "Outside of a few run-ins with some suppliers, it's been going pretty smoothly from what I can tell."

"Has he started building yet?" Simon asked. "I can't wait to see what Thomas does with that plot of land, it has an amazing view."

"He's finally leveled the land, and he said the foundation for the building will start as soon as the geothermal earth tube exchangers are in place," Josh beamed. "But don't ask me anything about it, I can't even begin to tell you all of the steps that go into such a huge construction project. I glanced at the plans the other night, and I couldn't believe the number of permits, tradespeople, and steps that are necessary."

Simon laughed, "I remember the headaches in getting Oliver's apartment suite over the garage ready for him to live in. If it wasn't for Wayne, I don't think I ever would have finished."

Josh smiled at the mention of his brother's name, "Wayne would've found the entire complex fascinating. He would have shown up every Saturday, hammer in hand, ready to work."

"There isn't a day that doesn't go by that I don't think of him," Simon said, speaking before an awkward silence filled the room at the mention of Wayne's name.

"Me too," Josh said, and then raised the folder in the air. "I better get on the phone and see if any of these people remember seeing anything suspicious happening around the field over the last few days."

Josh patted the file on Simon's shoulder as he walked out of the room. Simon watched him leave, choking back the tears that came every time Wayne's name was mentioned. One way or the other they'd get through the pain that losing Wayne brought to their lives, and eventually they'd find a way to talk about their memories without feeling the sting of the loss. But for now, they'd focus on finding a name for the man that was discovered buried in Belvedere Field, and bring his killer to justice.

CHAPTER 4

The examination and autopsy left Kerry with proof that there were traces of an antiseptic cleanser and barbiturates along with a single chrysanthemum seed. The killer had put too much thought into the preparation of the victim's body, and Kerry knew that the single seed must hold some significance.

Every internet search on the flower returned a different array of information. Some Kerry was familiar with but held no significance to the recent murder. She knew it was a flower that was found in several colors, sizes, and countries. In addition to being a favorite garden plant, it was also a culinary accessory in some exotic dishes. The flower even seemed to hold royal status in Japan, something that was both new and interesting but irrelevant to her victim.

The one feature that stood out in all her searches was that the flower became a symbol of death in the 17th Century.

This, Kerry determined, was more than just a coincidence. Her thoughts tumbled over scenarios as to why the victim would have been buried in a field after being meticulously cleansed with a disinfectant and with a single chrysanthemum seed lodged under one nail.

She couldn't recall finding a victim in such a state and wondered what would compel such a ritual.

She began entering phrases and questions into her internet search browser and reading as many entries as possible, hoping to find a clue that could connect the seed to a murder victim. As she read, she tapped her finger on the edge of her keyboard, paused, and then typed two additional words into the search bar.

Her eyes widened at the information that scrolled down the screen and she knew she was on the right path. She picked up her phone, dialed Simon's number, and began to speak before he had a chance to say hello.

"I need you to look something up for me," Kerry blurted into the phone.

"Did you find something during your autopsy?" Simon asked and Kerry could hear the door closing in his office.

"The victim was given a heavy dose of a barbiturate that rendered him unconscious, but it was the cut across his throat that killed him," Kerry explained. "His body had been completely wiped clean with a disinfectant, one that contained the same compounds that are used in hospitals before surgery."

"Completely washed?" Simon asked.

"Hair, skin, and even the inside of his mouth. But that's not what prompted me to call you. I also found a seed under his nail."

"What kind of seed?"

"A chrysanthemum seed," Kerry said. "Just one."

"That's a common flower, he could've picked it up anywhere."

"Not with the vigorousness that his body was cleansed and since the field is only filled with prairie grass, it must have been placed there intentionally. Plus, it's early spring so there's also no chance that our victim happened upon a flower gone to seed when he was killed."

That brought them to the reason for Kerry's request.

"What was it you wanted me to search for you?" Simon asked.

"The seed might be some sort of calling card, and the disinfectant could be a ritual that the killer used in the past with other victims."

"You think this could be a serial killer?"

If Simon was sitting across from Kerry he would have seen the doubt in her eyes. Hearing Simon vocalize the two words that she typed into the search browser made her reconsider her thoughts.

"I'm not sure," Kerry said. "But when I thought about the other remains that were found in the same field, it occurred to me that the same person could be responsible. What if they had killed and buried a previous victim there?"

"I guess it's possible," Simon said, but his tone didn't hold the same confidence his words did.

Kerry continued to explain, "After I typed in the term serial killer into the internet browser, I found an article about calling cards that are often left behind by some murderers."

"I'm aware of the concept, but I've never investigated a serial killing in Lake Pines."

"It could be the first murder of its kind, but I thought I'd have you check the police files. At the very least, you can rule out any connection to another crime."

There was a brief silence on the line before Simon began to enter some search parameters into the police database on his computer.

Kerry looked at the photograph of the victim that was open on her computer screen and she imagined the person he was before he was killed. He looked like someone who could've been a friend, someone who wouldn't have raised any alarms if he stepped close to her at the grocery store or in line at the bank. He wouldn't have been someone she would've pulled Dominique away from either.

"Did you find a name for our victim yet?" Kerry said interjecting Simon's search and both of their thoughts.

"Not yet, but Sally distributed the photo to every officer and they're asking around town to see if anyone recognizes him."

Kerry tried to imagine what his name would be but wasn't able to come up with anything that fit. She just hoped that they'd find out soon.

"I found something in our files, but I don't know how much it'll help," Simon said. "There was a case that the department closed in 1974. An investigation spanned across the province and lasted almost three years.

Victims were killed in the same manner that you're describing."

Kerry straightened her body and sat up in her chair, "How similar?"

"Each victim was washed with a harsh disinfectant and there was a deep cut across their necks."

"And the seed? Does it mention anything about a seed being placed under a nail?"

"Yeah, in fact, it was all of those things that linked the victims together. Once the killer was caught for one murder, he was charged with all of them."

"How many victims were there?"

"Five that the authorities knew of. The guy they arrested always claimed he was innocent and that his trial was rushed along because of public pressure."

"Who was arrested?"

"His name is Kaylum Randall," Simon said. "He was arrested after a witness identified him as the man who left a bar with one of the victims. A security camera outside the bar filmed him helping the girl into the cab of his truck before they drove away. She appeared intoxicated and unable to stand on her own. Not many businesses had security cameras back then but the bar had been robbed three times that year and the owner put a camera in and scanned it every night hoping to find the person who robbed him."

"Did he ever explain why he prepared the bodies the way he did?"

"No, in fact, he claimed he was innocent through his trial, which didn't last very long. There was a lot of public pressure to make an arrest and since he was the last person to be seen with the victim and had no alibi for the other murders, he was found guilty and sentenced to life in prison."

"Did he ever appeal the case?"

"Twice, but lost both times."

"And he never admitted to the killings?"

"No. In fact, he continued to claim his innocence even after he was sent to prison. But once he was arrested the killings stopped."

"That could only mean a few things. He either had an accomplice, or there's a copycat killer," Kerry said.

Then Simon said the one thing that every law enforcement officer feared, "Or Kaylum Randall was innocent."

CHAPTER 5

Kerry could almost feel the weight of guilt, or innocence if that were the case, tighten around her chest. Evidence, whether it was in the form of a fingerprint at a crime scene or a microscopic fiber found on a victim, guided investigations either away from suspects or toward them.

Both circumstances had life-altering consequences.

The worst outcomes that filled Kerry's thoughts were individuals who were falsely imprisoned and guilty criminals who walked free.

Shortly after she returned home, she grabbed the dog's leash and headed for the door. Before she could relax for the evening, she had to shift a space between her workday and her private life but three blocks into her walk her mind wandered back to the file she read just before she left her lab.

A bar's video surveillance unit had captured Kaylum Randall helping an inebriated woman into the passenger seat of his truck. The video evidence that recorded Kaylum with the serial killer's latest victim was the break that investigators were hoping for. The officers were hunting a serial killer who had expertly evaded capture for several years and finding the video with Kaylum and a victim was the closest the police had come to closing in on the person responsible. But once Kerry dug deeper into the file that summarized the investigation that led to Kaylum Randall's arrest, she realized there were two alternate suspects that the police were also investigating. But it was the presence of the chrysanthemum seed and a reclusive man's interest in gardening that locked Kaylum permanently into the sightline of the prosecutor.

Other than that, Kerry wasn't convinced that there was enough evidence against Kaylum Randall to pursue a charge let alone a conviction. It took the judge only a few hours to conclude Kaylum's guilt and Kerry wondered if the judge was sitting across from her today, would he reach the same decision.

The added pressure of the provincial election brought rise to the public's cry for a harder stance on crime. Candidates, eager to win votes, vowed to put an end to the fear that recent crimes had caused. Behind the scenes, the existing politicians pushed hard to have the murder investigation closed, knowing that an arrest in a high-profile serial murder investigation during the election could ensure their candidate's electoral success.

Kaylum Randall was arrested, stood trial, and ultimately convicted of five murders.

Kerry recounted the contents of the file as she walked down the street, distracted by her thoughts and unaware of the squirrel that dashed across their path.

Raven lurched forward, tightening the leash that was wrapped around Kerry's fingers, jolting her back from her thoughts of the murder victim.

However, as Kerry strolled by the florist shop, the thought of chrysanthemums and Kaylum Randall returned to her thoughts. And then subsequently to the trial that determined his fate. Those were the thoughts that Kerry struggled with when her autopsies were used to determine a suspect's innocence or guilt. It was a hazard in her job that she still wasn't comfortable with.

Kerry turned north and jogged toward the covered waterfront pavilion, tugging Raven behind her. Murals created by local artists were being displayed at an evening exhibition, and she hoped the distraction would quiet her thoughts.

The open-air street exhibit had been a combined effort from the Lake Pines Gallery and the youth center to promote talent that didn't fall squarely into the model of acceptable art. In other words, art that didn't easily sell to the mass market.

Talented artists who expressed their graphic arts prowess by tagging buildings and railway cars were given a formal platform where they could display their work without the threat of censorship or arrest. Under the vaulted pavilion, artists as young as twelve displayed their colorful swirls and strokes that represented their view of the world around them. Often ignored, the underrepresented group was able to express themselves proudly and openly. The theme of the exhibit, ironically, was innocence.

Kerry stood behind the crowd that assembled to watch a live demonstration of one of the young artists at work. Absorbed by the artist's talent, Kerry was lulled into a trance and for twenty minutes she thought of nothing else but the colors on the canvas in front of her and what they represented to the young girl painting them.

Interested onlookers asked the young artist questions about her work. At first, her voice shook, but the longer she talked about her paintings her nervousness fell away and she realized the interest and curiosity of the people standing around her were genuine. Her current painting featured elements of family and tradition and how exterior influences can alter the natural course of their growth.

During many investigations, it was something that Kerry often thought of when lives were cut short because of violence. It amazed Kerry how the artist was able to use certain colors and images to evoke those same emotions.

As the crowd dispersed, Kerry did too, weaving her way through the art displays as she headed to the far end of the pavilion. Her hand reached up to stifle a yawn as she emerged from under the cover of the dome, and she quickened her pace. The sun had almost set, and she wanted to return home in time to give Dominique a bath and read her a bedtime story. A ritual she looked forward to at the end of each day.

"You're Doctor Dearborne, right?"

Kerry was startled by the voice, and she yanked on Raven's leash as she turned around. Her affable grin shifted into the protected guard that always came when she was around reporters. Without responding to Harry Beale's question, Kerry turned back around and rushed up the hill toward Main Street.

"I just want to ask you a few questions," Harry pleaded as he followed Kerry up the hill. Raven lunged forward and growled, the reporter's quick movements were a little too fast for the dog's liking. "Whoa!" Harry stepped back, holding both of his hands up in the air, "I really just want to ask you a few questions, and if I don't get a story in by the end of the week the editor is going to have my neck."

Kerry's wariness toward the reporters at the local paper stemmed from one specific incident. And that reporter and the ensuing lawsuit were what came to mind when she was approached by anyone working for The Lake Pines Daily News.

Because of that, Kerry avoided speaking with reporters about cases and referred all inquiries to the police department's public relations representative whose approach was more professional and polite.

"You know the drill Harry, contact the police department," Kerry pulled Raven toward her body, not wanting to take the chance that he would lunge at the unwelcomed reporter who, she knew, was just doing his job.

"Please," the young reporter begged. "Just a few words on what's happening at Belvedere Field."

"Nothing that I'm at liberty to discuss."

"So, there *was* a body found," Harry's eyes widened.

"As I said," Kerry began.

"Yeah, I know, contact the police department," Harry's shoulders slumped forward, and he shoved his hands into his folded arms. "I just want to know if what Gary Fredricks said is true. Was there a murder victim found buried in Belvedere Field?"

Kerry let out a deep breath, trying to summon the calmness she felt when she watched the young artist paint just moments ago.

“If you could just confirm or deny what Gary Fredricks told me, then I’ll leave,” the reporter said.

“Yes, there was a body found.”

“Mr. Fredricks also said that the man they found was murdered in the last few days.” The reporter leaned forward and then asked, “Is that true?”

“What happened to one question?” Kerry snapped.

“Well, at least tell me this, was the victim shot, stabbed, or bludgeoned to death?”

And then Kerry said the one thing she had been thinking - but knew she shouldn’t say.

CHAPTER 6

It was the sales clerk at Timber Grove Lumber that recognized the image of the man that was found in Belvedere Field. Paul Morrow was a delivery driver for the local lumber store that had been in operation for over fifty years. Everyone who knew Paul agreed that he was a hard worker and easy to get along with.

Paul was thirty-three and had worked as a driver for almost four years. He lived in a small house on the edge of town close to Hilly Lake.

Josh offered to inform Paul's family of his death. Wayne's murder and the memory of hearing those painful words over the phone, even though they were coming from a friend, were still raw in Josh's memory.

Too many survivors are devastated by learning of the death of a loved one from the media, and the least Josh could do was to deliver the news with a modicum of understanding. Because of his personal experience, he was prepared for the onslaught of emotion that was certain to wash over Paul's family. He knew he'd be able to deliver the news empathetically since he could still remember the feeling he experienced when he learned of Wayne's death.

Hearing about the death of someone you care about is shocking enough, but finding out they were murdered burned deeply on an unimaginable level. And that was a pain that no words could prevent.

When Simon called on the day that Wayne was shot, Josh felt as if he had been pushed off a cliff. He was paralyzed by Simon's words and unable to speak or move. A million words of protest circulated through his mind but none came to his lips. His questions remained silent for the first few minutes while he absorbed Simon's explanation. Still, to this day, Josh wasn't sure that Simon could have approached the situation any differently.

The painful job of informing a family member of the death of a loved one rested uneasily on most officers' minds. Josh, however, understood the pain and believed that he could express the compassion necessary in the face of such an unspeakable tragedy.

At least that's what he hoped as he walked up the steps to the small bungalow on the edge of town.

The door swung open on the third knock and Josh was greeted by a laugh and then an apology, "I'm sorry. I thought you were my brother. Can I help you?"

Her jet black hair was long and tangled in a drooping bun that struggled to remain steady at the back of her head. Her hair moved as she spoke and a loose strand dangled in front of her left eye. A bright shade of yellow streaked the tip of her nose and the front of her shirt. She giggled as she spoke, and Josh suspected that habit would end once she realized why he was standing on the front step.

Yes, she lived in the house.

No, she wasn't Paul's sister, she was his fiancée.

Impulsively the young girl answered Josh's questions with a smile, but when she realized that he was a police officer and then recognized the solemn look in his eyes, her smile faded and the rosy color drained from her face.

The scream came in two waves. First from the depths of her gut, surging in the space between them, and then it grew deeper and more painful. As Josh looked at her face, it was her eyes that were yelling as the sound bypassed his ears and stabbed at his heart. She reached out and grasped the door frame as her legs collapsed from beneath her and Josh caught her just before her body hit the ground.

He guided the young woman to a chair inside her living room which was covered with drop cloths and a powerful scent of latex paint.

He held her hand, calming her down from her initial grief when she believed Paul had an accident to the terror that engulfed her when she learned he had been murdered. He explained what happened, although he was careful to do so with limited details.

Bethany Wessex had moved into the house a few months before Paul proposed and their wedding was planned for the middle of June.

"Is there anyone I can call for you, Bethany?" Josh asked.

She shook her head and then raised her watery eyes to meet Josh's as she changed her mind, "Maybe my parents."

Bethany sat motionless in the chair as Josh made the call to her parents. A hollow echo filled the space, where just moments ago, a large smile and bright green eyes had happily greeted him. It was the familiar blank noise that draped awkwardly over everyone that learned of a loved one's death.

Josh insisted on waiting until Bethany's parents arrived. He didn't want to leave her alone knowing she'd only ask herself questions she had no way of answering. And even though Josh had more information than she did about Paul's death, he wasn't sure his answers would bring Bethany comfort.

"Why?" Bethany asked. Tears puddled at the corner of her mouth, cascading down her cheeks before they fell from the edge of her slim jaw.

Josh handed Bethany a tissue, offering the standard response that was given to all family members, "I don't know Bethany, but I can promise you that we will do everything in our power to find the person responsible for Paul's death."

"Was it a robbery?"

Again, Josh offered words of sympathy but explained that it was too early in the investigation to know for certain what lead to Paul's death.

"When was the last time you spoke with Paul?" Simon asked.

"When he left three days ago," Bethany dragged her hand under her nose and pushed back a sob. "We had breakfast together before he left for his trip."

"Where did he go?"

"He was heading up north to make some deliveries. Sometimes he's in areas with no cell reception so I don't always hear from him when he's on the road," Bethany explained. "He wasn't supposed to return until tomorrow. That's why my brother was coming by, he was going to help me get the room painted before Paul got home."

Bethany's shoulders slumped forward, her hollow eyes darted around the room, "It took us a week to agree on a color."

Josh was about to make a comment about how nice the paint looked on the wall, but his lips pressed closed. The compliment seemed odd given the circumstances. He rested his hand on

Bethany's arm at the same moment her mother ran through the door, with her father trailing close behind. Both of their eyes were stained red from crying.

Despondent and terrified with the news of how Paul died, Josh left Bethany in the care of her parents and promised to contact them if there were any developments in the investigation.

"I'll send an officer by to bring you to identify his body when you're ready," Josh said just before he left.

Throughout the day Josh was able to put together a picture of who Paul Morrow was. Kind, friendly, hard-working, and eager to start a family with Bethany. Bethany gave Josh the names of Paul's friends, favorite shops, and restaurants as he prepared to retrace his steps and figure out where he may have encountered his killer.

He dialed Simon's number and filled him in on the events of the morning.

"That must have been difficult, Josh," Simon consoled his friend.

"His fiancée was devastated to learn about Paul's death. But she confirmed what his coworkers at Timber Grove Lumber had said. Paul was an easy guy to work with, there were never any customer complaints against him, and his work record was spotless. He was even up for a promotion," Josh said. "I got a list of the businesses that Paul made deliveries to over the last month. Maybe that'll point us in the direction of someone who may have seen something that can help us."

"How long is the list?" Simon asked.

"Three pages long."

"Do you want some help with contacting the people and businesses on the list?"

"No, I'll be fine. Bethany did mention that she thought Paul was up north making some deliveries for Timber Grove Lumber and that she wasn't expecting him home until tomorrow. The supervisor at his work didn't mention that so I'll swing by on my way back to the station and see if I can get some information on the delivery route," Josh said. "But that means I won't be able to meet you today to help with the ground-penetrating radar machine."

"I'm not sure if I'm going to be able to do anything but stand around and watch anyway," Simon admitted. "I've never needed to use equipment like this in any investigation so I'll probably be pretty useless. Just work on the list you have and when I'm done I'll swing by the station and we can compare notes."

"Sounds good," Josh said and then ended the call.

Josh drove directly to Timer Grove Lumber to speak with Paul's boss. He found him behind the front desk comforting an employee who had just learned of Paul's death. Several other employees were huddled together to the side of the counter, and a few were trying to look busy by stocking shelves as they wiped tears from their eyes. Josh nodded his head toward the few employees that looked directly at him and he motioned to the manager who stepped aside to speak with Josh privately.

"I know this is a difficult time for you," Josh said, trying to soften the sting of his return. "But I was wondering if I could get the name of the companies Paul was making deliveries to this week."

"Paul wasn't making any deliveries for us for the last few days," the manager said. "He asked for a few days off to take care of some personal things before the summer."

"Are you certain?" Josh asked.

"Positive. I'm the one who makes the schedules for all of the employees. If Paul was making any deliveries, the orders would have gone through me first."

Josh left Timber Grove Lumber and drove back into Lake Pines, focusing on what could have transpired in the days before Paul's murder. But no matter how hard he tried to stop them, images of Wayne passed across his mind and the emotion he was pushing down for several months suddenly erupted into a flood of tears.

Josh pulled the car over to the side of the road and leaned his head against the steering wheel.

He had stopped crying in front of Lucia shortly after Wayne's funeral, hoping to help his daughter realize that life would go on, even though losing Wayne drove a chasm into their lives.

Unable to hold in his tears, he pulled over and allowed himself ten minutes at the side of the road, releasing the sadness that he could no longer suppress. Strangely, it was eight minutes longer than he had allowed himself to grieve since Wayne was buried.

And he knew it wasn't long enough.

Josh wiped the tears from his face and cleared his throat. He steered the car back onto the highway and headed back into Lake Pines, vowing to help Bethany find some peace in the madness of Paul's murder. And the first thing he needed to do was to find out why Paul Morrow lied about being out of town.

CHAPTER 7

Simon parked beside Belvedere Field and waved to the man leaning against a white pickup truck. He was wearing a long-sleeved shirt and thick work pants – and except for his boots, he was dressed entirely in black. His hands were folded as he rested them against the top of his forehead, shielding his eyes from the sun as he looked down onto the field.

Tents were raised just before the two-hour heavy downpour that came following the exhumation of Paul Morrow's body. Today, however, the storm clouds had cleared, and the vivid hues of early spring returned to the field along with the melodic tune of nesting robins. The shift to milder weather would make the search easier, even though the previous day's rain left the ground soggy and muddy puddles filled the divets in the ground.

Simon wasn't sure what to expect when he arrived at Belvedere Field, but as Peter promised, the ground-penetrating radar machine arrived along with a technician who was trained to operate it. This, Simon surmised, was the man looking down onto the field standing next to the truck with the provincial police logo stamped on the door.

The machine was slightly larger than a lawnmower and reminded Simon of an android machine that belonged in a science fiction film.

A quick introduction and a brief explanation gave the technician the information he needed before he started his scan of the field. The technician, Gavin Rollins, was not only the person in charge of operating the machine, he was also the brains behind the development of the high-tech computer software. Initially, Gavin worked as an independent contractor, hired out by private businesses, construction firms, and various police departments around the province. When the police department realized how quickly their search budget was being depleted by hiring Gavin on a per-case basis, they brought him on as a full-time employee at half the cost. Which also gave them full access to his time and the ground-penetrating radar machine.

"That's the machine?" Simon asked, pointing to the white and black unit that Gavin lowered down the ramp of his truck.

"Yeah, this baby has seen it all," Gavin patted his hand on the screen that was mounted to the handles. "What area do you want me to cover?"

Simon looked out on the five acres and then down at the small machine and wondered if the compact unit was up to the task of scanning the entire field.

"Let's start with the space inside the yellow tape, specifically focusing on the area where we already dug," Simon guided Gavin to a mound of soil and a partially dug hole. "It rained yesterday afternoon so the ground will be a bit muddy in spots."

The officer standing next to the unearthed ground removed the tarp and wooden marker that pinpointed where Paul Morrow's body was found.

"That's not a problem, the unit is outfitted with all-terrain tires. I've even used this machine over thick layers of snow and ice."

Confident that Gavin knew what he was doing, Simon stood to the side and watched as the machine purred to life. Working in a straight line, Gavin scanned the ground moving from east to west, and then back again. Following the lines on the screen that also mapped out the field's uneven terrain, Gavin moved over the ground at a slow, steady pace, saving the images onto a USB stick.

Every dip in the ground, dense patch of rock, lost coins, and long roots from nearby trees were all mapped out on the screen.

Gavin slowed his pace as he reached the location of Paul Morrow's shallow grave and the spot where Simon had informed him that a bone from another body was also found. As Gavin moved the machine over the ground, green wavy lines jiggled across the screen, outlining an image that lay deep inside the earth.

Below their feet, a skeleton was stretched flat.

"Can you tell far down the body is?" Simon asked.

Gavin leaned forward, calculated the computer readings, and then looked up, "About six feet. The bone was probably pushed up with the repeated freezing and thawing of the soil."

It wasn't the first body that Gavin had found while using the ground-penetrating radar machine, however, since he had been hired to work full-time for the province he had seen more than he cared to remember.

The first body Gavin found was during the scan of a future construction site in downtown Toronto six years ago. The remains were that of a lawyer who had disappeared on his way home from a business meeting. The man was a partner at one of the city's established law practices and the meeting was with the CEO of a new tech firm who was accused of misappropriation of funds. It was always assumed the lawyer had met his demise because of what he learned at that meeting, but any evidence was purely circumstantial and no charges were ever laid.

When they found the lawyer's body, he had been buried along with his briefcase which contained the evidence necessary to charge the CEO in question. That was the day that Gavin realized that some good could be found with the use of his machine and he approached several police departments in the province, informing them of the usefulness of his compact ground-penetrating radar machine.

Gavin pushed the machine forward, then he abruptly stopped and turned his face toward Simon, "There's another hit."

Simon walked up beside the machine and looked at the screen. Each step fell awkwardly now that he was aware of the second body that lay below their feet. The additional skeleton was positioned in the same fashion. It too was lying flat in the ground at a depth of at least six feet.

Simon motioned for Gavin to continue, and watched the screen as the image of another skeleton came into view less than two feet away.

The three bodies lay next to each other, spread at equal distances and buried at the same depth.

Simon looked at Gavin and then to the second officer who was standing nearby and noticed the same look of shock on their faces.

No one spoke, as they looked to each other for some explanation for what they were seeing on the screen. Simon swallowed and nervously asked Gavin to continue scanning.

Soon it was apparent that what they found was not just random bodies buried in an empty field. Looking down the length of the property and beyond to the dark water that rushed along the shoreline, Simon realized they were standing on an unmarked graveyard.

CHAPTER 8

Thirty-one bodies were buried in the vacant lot that most people in Lake Pines referred to as Belvedere Field. No one knew where the name came from and even though there was never a sign indicating that was the official name of the field, the designation stuck.

Belvedere Field had been the location of many family picnics, community gatherings, and small weddings. Now it possessed the unpleasant distinction of being the location of a large field with several unmarked graves.

Simon asked Kerry to meet him at Belvedere Field but waited until she arrived before he revealed the number of remains they found. He waited for her at the top of the hill, just out of sight of the field, and prepared her for what she was about to see.

In addition to the additional police tape used to mark off a larger section of the field, wooden stakes marked the position where the skull for each body lay below the ground. Looking from the top of the hill, Kerry thought the scene reminded her of several black and white Remembrance Day images of rushed burials in battlefields.

The graves lay alongside each other, each row the same distance from the next one. The absence of coffins was the reason a bone was visible when the body of Paul Morrow was exhumed. The level of decomposition and the condition of the bones proved the buried remains were distinctly older. This differentiated the murder of Paul Morrow from the remains concealed below.

"It was a strange coincidence that whoever buried Paul Morrow in this field just happened to choose an area where bodies were previously buried," Simon said as he stood next to Kerry watching the slow excavation. "Without it, we may never have known this massive grave existed."

"I brought Dominique here for a picnic with my dad last summer," Kerry said thinking back to the warm sunny day that was now spoiled with the knowledge that there were bodies buried below them the entire time.

"It could be an old gravesite from before the town was even settled," Simon suggested, believing it would make finding a large number of remains less disturbing. "We'll know more once you have a chance to examine the remains."

"I'll let you know what I find," Kerry pulled her keys out of her pocket. "I'll go to the lab and get ready. In the meantime, have the first set of remains transported there and hold off on removing any of the others until we have an idea of what we're looking at. We might want to get a larger forensic team to work on the removal of the bones."

"I contacted Peter and he's putting a rush on releasing the owner's name for the property. I keep running into roadblocks. Each time I research a company, it leads to another corporation that has gone out of business or has changed names."

Before she turned to leave, Kerry took one last glance at the field, crowded with wooden stakes and surrounded by yellow tape. She knew Simon would remain at the site for the remainder of the day, not wanting to leave until he had a clearer picture of what lay buried beneath the field.

Sadness was something Simon had difficulty disguising and the knowledge of the thirty-one bodies beneath the layers of soil on Belevedere Field would weigh on his heart and consume his thoughts.

Simon wanted to believe that they were simple graves, innocently buried and forgotten with time and where the harsh weather had either rotted or destroyed the grave markers. But thirty-one bodies was too large a number to bury unnoticed.

With no one but the Lake Pines police to investigate, Simon would take on the responsibility to find the truth, and at least Kerry knew it was something she could help him with once she began to examine the first set of remains.

She returned to her lab and prepared the area for the first examination. Having completed Paul Morrow's autopsy, the investigation into his murder was now in the hands of the police department, and she knew the next natural step would be for them to speak with Kaylum Randall. The man who may, or may not be, innocent of the crimes he was sentenced to many years earlier.

Kerry was ready when the first set of remains arrived at her lab. The glaring detail that struck Kerry was the fact that none of the bodies were buried in coffins.

Wrapped in a partially disintegrated canvas cloth, the remains were lowered into the ground and displayed as if they were buried ceremonially. However, the absence of coffins and grave markers led her to believe that these weren't official burials.

Nondescript blue pants, thick and frayed from years underground were still wrapped around the bottom half of the body. The shirt, made of a thinner material had not fared as well and had mostly disintegrated exposing the decomposed remains.

Stained from the dark mineral-rich mud, the bones were fragile and thin cracks marked the surfaces of the skeleton. Closer inspection would determine which cracks were caused by injuries and which were marked by the assault of time.

Kerry ran her fingers over the frail bones, shocked at how small they were. The person that lay before her was no taller than five feet and the small bone structure indicated that this was a child who had not yet reached puberty. The boy's skull was intact and Kerry was certain her facial reconstruction software could generate a reasonable likeness of what he looked like just before he died. She could use the estimated size of the clothing to determine the boy's heft, although, on initial inspection of the clothes, there didn't seem to be much room for extra weight.

She removed the frayed material carefully, trying not to damage it any further, and placed them on an evidence table next to the body. Very carefully, she began to wash the bones, brushing away thick hardened clumps of mud and dirt that had adhered to the joints and surfaces.

Her brush pushed against the dirt, slowly sweeping away grains of sand, small stones, and pieces of mud until the bone was exposed. Working down the length of the arm, the hairs on the brush snagged on the wrist joint.

Kerry pulled the arm of the magnifying glass close to the body and pulled the strands out of the joint, careful not to damage the skeleton.

As she lifted the brush a large clump of dirt fell away exposing something more than the small wrist bone that she expected to see.

It was a small beaded bracelet, held together with a strand of leather and covered in hardened clay from the ground. As Kerry washed away the dirt, the colors on the small plastic beads came to life. Three shades of blue mixed with a few red and yellow beads. It was impossible to ignore the innocence and youth that the small colorful bracelet represented. A rush of emotion grasped Kerry. The bracelet was a handmade craft, possibly a sense of pride for the child, and the simplicity and innocence represented the life that created it. Kerry carefully set it aside on the evidence table next to the body.

With the unearthed skeleton fully exposed, Kerry paused and glanced down at the bones. They were arranged as if the child was still sleeping. Peaceful and in the midst of a dream. Kerry's thoughts went to her own daughter, Dominique, and wondered what tragedy had befallen this boy to find him lowered into an early grave without a coffin to cradle him or a gravestone to acknowledge his life.

Leaning forward, she examined the bones making note of the cracks that streaked the surface. A break on the collarbone had completely mended and was marked with the bone callus that formed in its place. A larger break on the femur had not been set properly and had healed slightly off-center, likely causing a limp in the boy's final days.

Both breaks, although painful to experience, would not have been the reason for the child's death. She wanted to take a closer look before testing the bone and pulled the scanning machine toward the table, extending the levered arm over the body, lining up the red dot in the center of his torso. She pressed the green button and the machine purred to life as it slowly moved over the table, scanning the bones below.

A series of images flashed across her computer and slowly and carefully Kerry examined each slide.

In addition to small stress fractures that were visible in the wrists and ankles, there were mild osteological signs of malnutrition. Kerry reached for her instruments and extracted a sample of bone from the femur.

While she waited for the results of the tests, she picked up the bracelet. Holding it between her fingers, she moved it around trying to find some marking that could tell her what the child's name was. But she found none.

The whirring sound of the printer echoed in the empty lab as it printed the results of the tests. Mycobacterium tuberculosis as well as elevated levels of lead were present in the bone samples.

This was most likely the cause of death for the young child. As difficult as it was to look down at the forgotten bones of a small child, Kerry was relieved that the remains were not connected to a murder. She could focus on determining when the boy was buried and identify him and the other bodies with the death certificates registered in the province.

Identifying the remains that were found in the unknown grave, in a nondescript and forgotten graveyard was an easier task than facing the prospect of another murder.

CHAPTER 9

Josh arrived as Kerry was storing the remains and filing the computer printouts.

"Simon is still at Belvedere Field coordinating the protection of the site," Josh handed Kerry a cup. "I stopped by Lisa's and picked up a coffee for you. I thought you might need it."

Kerry thanked him and explained the findings of her examination.

"So that means it's not a murder we're investigating," Josh said. "At least that's something."

“Is there any idea yet who owns the property?” Kerry asked.

Josh shook his head, “We should know by tomorrow morning since Peter is using his pull to get us a name. I always thought that field was part of the forest, I had no idea that it was privately owned.”

“Considering the amazing view, it’s odd that no one ever built on the property,” Kerry said but then it occurred to her that if the owner was aware of the bodies that were buried in the field, that would’ve been reason enough to avoid building on the property.

Josh’s face indicated he was thinking the same thing. “It’s likely that the owner leased the field to the town if they needed a cemetery.”

But as the words left Josh's mouth he realized how unlikely that scenario was.

"How long ago do you think the bodies were buried in the field?" Josh asked.

"Assuming they were all buried around the same time, around forty-five to fifty years ago. I'll be sure once I get the bones carbon-dated."

"Wayne and I weren't even born yet," Josh leaned back in his chair. "But it's not that long ago, you'd think that something would have appeared in the register when Simon checked to see who the owner is."

"Which means that the burials may not have been official."

As they both thought of the ramifications of Kerry's last statement, they sat quietly figuring out what they would do next.

"I used my facial recognition software to generate a likeness of the young boy," Kerry pulled a sheet out of the file and handed it to Josh. "Plus there was this."

Kerry held out her hand, the small beaded bracelet resting in the center of her palm.

"Seeing that bracelet reminds you that the boy was so young," Josh said.

Kerry returned the bracelet to the evidence bag on her desk. "Any updates on Paul Morrow's investigation?"

"I'm halfway through the list of businesses on his delivery route and so far, nothing seems suspicious."

"Simon said that you volunteered to go out and speak with his fiancée?"

Josh nodded.

"How are you doing after that?" Kerry asked.

"It was difficult, but I felt I'd be the right person to deliver the news since I can relate to her situation."

"Do you think that Kaylum Randall was innocent all along?" Kerry asked. It had been the question on her mind since she read the file on the murder investigation.

Josh shrugged his shoulders, "There are other possibilities why the murder of Paul Morrow is similar to the serial murders that Kaylum Randall was arrested for in 1974. The most likely being that he had an accomplice."

"If his accomplice was close to Kaylum's age that would put him around 70. Why would he have stayed so silent all of these years?"

"He could've been out of town, or even arrested for another charge altogether,"

Josh said. "We won't know until we find the person responsible."

"You read the file, what do you think?" Kerry asked. "Do you think the police arrested the right person? Kaylum Randall always said he was innocent."

"Yeah, he and most of the men on his cell block. Even without direct DNA evidence linking him to the murder, he was seen in areas where the five women were murdered, plus, he didn't have an alibi for the nights the women went missing. When the police showed up at his home to question him about being seen with the final victim at the bar, they found a greenhouse in his backyard," Josh paused. "Do you want to guess what he was growing?"

"Chrysanthemums?"

Josh nodded.

"Thousands of people grow flowers, Josh, that doesn't make them serial killers."

"No, but there was a lot of circumstantial evidence along with mounting public pressure to make an arrest. But one thing is certain, there were no particulars reported in the news, so there is no way this is just a copycat crime perpetrated by someone looking to get some attention." Josh pointed his finger at Kerry, changing the topic, "By the way, I was surprised to find you were the one who spoke with Harry Beale about the body in Belvedere Field."

"I was in the wrong place at the wrong time, or so the saying goes," Kerry tried to make light of the well-known fact that she avoids reporters at all costs. "He caught me off guard and asked about the body."

Josh shook his head, "Sorry you got stuck with that, but I have to commend you on doing a pretty good job."

Harry had blocked Kerry's path as she left the artist exhibit under the pavilion, peppering her with questions about the body found in the popular field. She avoided revealing the nature of Paul's death, or his name and just repeated that it was an active case that the killer would be caught soon.

"Maybe referring to the killer as a sick twisted weakling is a good indication that you wouldn't be the ideal spokesperson for the department," Josh laughed recalling the article in the morning paper.

"Not my most diplomatic response, but Harry wouldn't get out of my way," Kerry said, explaining the reason for her short temper with the reporter. "It was either that or let Raven take a piece out of him."

"No, that wouldn't have been a good idea," Josh laughed, drank the last part of his coffee, and tossed his cup in the recycling bin. "I'm going to get back to the office and finish with that list before I head home."

Kerry thanked Josh for the coffee and walked him to the door.

"Don't stay too late," Josh said as he pushed open the door. "I have a feeling it's going to be a busy few weeks with the recent investigations."

"I won't be too much longer, but I want to make sure I file everything away before I leave."

By the time Kerry completed her work, filed the necessary paperwork, and then left her lab it was already dark. She pulled into the driveway and parked along the row of hedges bordering their neighbor's lawn. The light above the garage was turned off, eliminating the bright yellow haze that normally filled the shadows along the side of the house. Safety was the main concern for Simon installing the motion-detected light fixture, but its constant glow disturbed Oliver's sleep and he'd turn it off every night, allowing him the peace and darkness to relax at the end of the day.

Kerry stepped out of the car, grabbed her bag from the back seat, and walked toward the house. She could see her father through the kitchen window as he held Dominique, and she rushed her steps toward the house when someone suddenly grabbed her from behind.

Kerry struggled, fighting against her attacker, her survival instincts kicking in as she pulled against the tightening grip.

She stumbled, falling back into her attacker's body, as his gloved hand squeezed tighter with each effort she made to break free. Kerry was unable to move her left arm as her attacker pulled her away from the house. If Oliver glanced out of the window at that moment, he would've seen the stranger pulling his daughter deeper into the shadows.

Away from the house, and away from her family.

Kerry stomped her feet, kicking them backward, landing her heel on the front of her attacker's shin, causing him to stumble and freeing his hand from her mouth. Kerry let out a scream just before she was pulled back.

Kerry could feel the pressure of her attacker's hand against her windpipe, closing off her airway. She could tell by the strength in his grip that it would take little effort for him to break her neck and permanently silence her cries for help. She was growing dizzy, and each swing of her right arm missed its intended target. Sounds were growing dull and it wasn't until Raven was on top of them that she also heard her father's shouts as he ran down the driveway.

The second scream she heard was not hers, but that of her attacker as Raven clamped down on his arm, tugging at his sleeve and pulling him away from Kerry.

As she scrambled to her feet, so did her attacker. He twisted his arm free from Raven's grip and ran down the driveway, disappearing into the night.

Raven ran after him as Oliver pulled Kerry from the ground and wrapped his arms around her. Raven's barks echoed into the stillness of the night with a fierceness Kerry had never heard before. As Raven ran further away and his barks disappeared into the darkness, Oliver pulled his daughter closer.

CHAPTER 10

Thomas slipped his arm through the safety vest as he walked along the edge of the water to the temporary construction office that was set up in the mobile trailer inside the fence. He arrived at the worksite an hour later than he normally did and his crew was already working on preparing the ground for the foundation.

Thomas purchased the property because of its unobstructed view of the lake, which was essential for the eco-friendly theme of the residential complex. Months of preparation went into two bids on various properties but his delay in securing the property meant he wouldn't be finished within the timeline he had planned. Plus a small environmental group was arguing against the new waterside development and their concerns threatened to stop the project before it even began.

When Thomas agreed to move from Toronto, he thought it would be the right decision for both their family and his career. Neither he nor Josh wanted to raise Lucia in a busy city, even if it was one that they loved. The social and entertainment aspects of living in Canada's largest city suit their lives. Along with the business opportunities that Thomas found, it was the city that he and Josh called home for several years.

However, comfort turned into caution when they were faced with the realities of raising a daughter in the downtown core. Their solution was to sell their condo and move slightly further north but to remain within the confines of the city limits. They settled into a neighborhood with trees, parks, and other families with young children. Schools and child care were close to their home, but both he and Josh longed for the serenity of the small-town life they were both raised in.

Sydney, Nova Scotia for Thomas, and Lake Pines, Ontario for Josh.

The opportunity to move to Lake Pines presented itself after Wayne had died. They had talked about relocating to a smaller town or city, and they agreed that once the best opportunity presented itself that they'd make the leap.

Josh had dealt with his brother's death better than Thomas had expected him to, which made their transition to Lake Pines much easier. They moved into Wayne's house, which was his and Josh's original family home, and they settled into a comfortable pattern in which Lucia thrived.

Had it not been for Thomas' frequent confrontations with their neighbor, Bill Gibbons, their move would have been seamless.

Usually, it was accusations of Thomas' truck being parked too close to the property line, the noise of the lawnmower on Saturday mornings, or the brightness of the motion detector light that prompted a complaint.

The former town councilor, armed with the knowledge of local by-laws, frequently harassed his neighbors. Wielding the firepower at almost every resident on the street.

Mid-sixties and flaunting an excessively bronzed hue, Bill Gibbons had a habit of speaking *at* people and not *with* them. Single and living alone since his daughter moved away to attend school, Bill's hobbies seemed to veer towards the insane such as extreme recycling and memorization of town by-laws.

This morning, as Thomas was leaving for work, it was the branch of a tree that extended over Bill's driveway that brought the latest grievance.

Bill threatened to remove the offending branch himself, but Thomas wasn't convinced that Bill wouldn't have haphazardly hacked the branch off the seventy-year-old tree just to prove a point. The best option, Thomas decided, was to trim the branch himself while former Councilor Gibbons supervised.

Thomas left the lopsided tree and his mildly appeased neighbor and rushed to the worksite.

The property adjacent to the marina wasn't Thomas' first choice, but in the end, it fit better with his design. Securing the necessary funding for the project had also presented an issue since the majority of investors completed a rigorous background search on Thomas' previous projects before they would agree to their financial involvement with his newest venture.

Reaching into the millions of dollars, Thomas knew that finding an investor that would trust in his work ethics and principles would be a challenge. Especially with the incident from Toronto that marred his record. Asking his lawyer to clear his name and defend the charges wasn't worth the effort since he knew that it would be almost impossible to counteract the allegations that were leveled against him. Evidence that brought the accusation into his life directly linked him to a crime, and he decided that the best course of action was to let the situation subside on its own. He avoided a court case by agreeing to a financial settlement, left the firm, and started his own business - free from the glare of condemning and judgmental eyes. The success of this new project would help him put the horrors of those years behind him, once and for all.

Thomas' first task, once he arrived at the worksite, was to speak with his foreman, Carlos Davila, who filled him in on the site's progress. He was waiting for Thomas in the small trailer that doubled as their office and planning room.

"We've almost completely cleared the area next to the water's edge. In a few days, we can begin to lay the foundation for the shoreline support," Carlos removed his bright yellow hardhat, scratched his head, and then placed it on the table. "After that, we can get the infrastructure planned out for the building."

"Has the inspector been here today? I want to make sure I'm around when he arrives," Thomas unrolled the blueprints on the table, placing a rock on each corner to prevent it from springing back into a tube.

Carlos shook his head, "Not yet. I think he is coming early this afternoon."

Carlos worked for Thomas in Toronto and jumped at the opportunity to move to Lake Pines to work on the specialized project. Once Thomas secured the financing, he contacted Carlos and they began to assemble the rest of their work crew.

Kind and reliable, Thomas learned shortly after he hired Carlos that he could entrust every aspect of his business to the thirty-year-old. Outside of an Audrey Hepburn tattoo on his arm, Carlos had never made a decision out of haste or without thinking it through.

"Have the quotes on the earth tube exchangers arrived from the manufacturer?" Thomas asked. "The city inspector said he wants all of the specifications on them before we begin, and I don't want any headaches with the city permits."

"Is that nutty neighbor of yours still giving you grief?" Carlos learned that Thomas' frustration with the city coincided with altercations with his neighbor.

"Yeah. That's why I was late today," Thomas explained. "I had to trim a branch from our tree that Bill complained was extended too far over onto his driveway."

"He had an issue with the branch?"

"More like the small new spring leaves that were falling to the ground and then staining his driveway."

"I still don't know why you don't tell Josh," Carlos said. "Having a cop as a husband should give you some pull."

"Josh has enough on his plate. Even though we agreed to not talk about work at home, I can tell he's been dealing with a tough case and the last thing he needs to deal with is our annoying neighbor."

Carlos shook his head, "That's why I'm renting an apartment. There are fewer issues with picky neighbors."

Thomas started to relax as the morning passed. The mild weather and the speed of the work crew put his mind at ease concerning the progress of the project. An email with the manufacturer's quote on the tube exchangers came in just before noon and was a few thousand dollars under what Thomas had budgeted. Leaving more money for the landscaping that would help attract buyers to the development, and he started to believe that things were looking up.

Thomas was repositioning a sign on the gate when the crunching of the gravel drew his attention to the cars pulling up to the property.

The flashing lights and the grim face of the officer stepping out of the car brought work at the construction site to a screeching halt.

Simon's walk was quick and each step measured, and even though he had a smile on his face, Thomas could sense the tension in his approach.

The delivery was quick and painful, "I'm sorry Thomas, I'm going to have to shut you down."

CHAPTER 11

The forensic team arrived and Simon cordoned off the property. Thomas stepped to the side but remained close enough to listen to the instructions Simon gave to each officer.

Attentively, Thomas took in each word and felt a numbness cross over him. This was Josh's zone. These were words and situations that were frequent components in Josh's workday. This wasn't the normal situation for a property developer, or at least, it wasn't supposed to be.

The body was found at the base of a hill on the eastern section of the property. It was the proposed site for the development's green space and was the current location for the site's landfill.

Ambulance sirens echoed off the wall of trees in the nearby forest and the deafening scream carried through the worksite.

"Is he alive?" Thomas interrupted Simon as he was speaking with two officers.

Simon shook his head, "The paramedics routinely arrive when 911 is called. I instructed that they make a silent approach, but the information doesn't always get relayed correctly."

"So, the person, or the body they found, is dead?" Thomas whispered, not sure what the ideal approach in a situation like this should be.

"I'm afraid so."

"What does that mean for my project?" Thomas asked. "Not to sound cold or anything."

Thomas immediately regretted the shallowness of his question. But any further delay on the project could give his investor the final reason they needed to pull their promise of funding.

"The man's death was no accident," Simon explained. "We'll need unrestricted access to the entire worksite so our forensic team can search for possible clues as to what happened here."

Thomas swallowed down, "What do you mean?"

"Unfortunately your development site is now the scene of a murder investigation."

Thomas dragged his hand across his face, his shaking palm was stained with streaks of dirt mingled with his nervous sweat. He lifted his gaze and looked past Simon and to the property leading down to the water. In the matter of a few months, the vacant property had gone from a serene field with a spectacular view to a scarred battlefield marked with trenches and large craters for their building's foundation and was now the grave of a murder victim.

"Give me a few minutes, then I have a few questions for you," Simon said before he walked toward the two officers waiting by the gate.

Thomas' head swirled, and he looked behind where he was standing and lowered himself into a chair next to the trailer. He waited an additional ten minutes while Simon spoke with the officers who were monitoring access to the site.

"No one gets in or out without their name being put on a list," Simon said.

The officers acknowledged the instructions with a nod and then Simon turned around and walked over to where Thomas was sitting.

"Sorry about that," Simon apologized. "I just want to make sure that everyone is accounted for."

"I understand."

But he didn't. Thomas didn't understand anything that was happening, and he figured that the questions Simon needed him to answer wouldn't make things any clearer.

"Who has access to the construction site after hours?"

"There are only two people with keys to the gate and this office," Thomas pointed to the gray trailer they were sitting beside. "Me and the foreman, Carlos Davila."

"I'm going to want to talk to him before I leave."

"You don't think one of my guys had anything to do with this murder, do you?" Thomas asked, panic settling into his words.

"I just want to have a clear understanding of who had access to the property after dark. It doesn't mean we believe you, or one of your employees had anything to do with the murder," Simon explained.

"Then why the question?" Thomas knew he sounded impatient and tried to soften his words by adding, "Just because I know my employees are going to ask me the same thing."

"The body was found inside the fence which is locked when you leave at the end of the day," Simon said. "The height of the fence combined with the position of the body means that the killer would have had to be inside the gate to reach the base of the hill where the body was found."

"How did you even know he was here?" Thomas asked. "Carlos unlocked the gate at seven-thirty and we haven't seen or heard anyone arrive before you did."

"The victim's girlfriend had traced his fitness tracker to this location," Simon said.

"You know who he is?"

Simon nodded, "Do you know anyone by the name of David Woodward? He's a personal trainer who does private fitness consultations. One of those one-on-one training programs that get people into shape with specialized exercises and diet."

"No, but then again I haven't met anyone outside of work or the small group of friends that Josh knows. What happened?"

"He didn't come home after his last appointment yesterday, and his girlfriend, Kori Bradford, couldn't reach him on his phone. She called the police but she was told to give it a bit more time before reporting David as a missing person. She didn't like that answer and logged onto his computer and began to track his fitness tracker, and that pointed here. It was one of those running devices that was embedded into the insole of his shoe, which is the only way we were able to locate him since his phone was discarded."

"Do you need anything from me?" Thomas asked.

"I'll need a complete list of your staff along with their contact information, as well as anyone else who may have had access to the construction site over the last few weeks."

"I'll print out a list of our employees with their phone numbers and then I'll go back in our log records and assemble a list of names of anyone else who was at the site," Thomas went into the trailer, turned on the computer and printed off the list of employees to give to Simon.

As the pages of names and phone numbers tumbled out of the printer, Thomas wondered how long he could keep the news of the murder investigation from his investor.

CHAPTER 12

Once back home, Thomas slumped into an oversized chair and closed his eyes. It was early afternoon and Lucia was still at school and Josh wouldn't be home for several hours, which gave him the quiet he needed to figure out what he was going to do.

Police officers would start interviewing his employees. Probing questions relating to a murder investigation were never easy to hear or to respond to, even for an innocent person.

The mere act of being questioned about your whereabouts would increase anyone's pulse. He reassured his staff that the temporary closure of the construction site wouldn't affect their jobs. Once the police concluded their investigation, they'd be back up and running.

At least Thomas hoped it was temporary.

For the last seven years, Thomas had pushed down the memory of the accusations that shattered his career and almost destroyed his life. Josh had stood by him during those stressful days and months and when Thomas could see no end in sight, Josh's outlook was always positive and bright.

Josh would always remind him - *Where one door closes, another always opens.* But now they had Lucia to protect which brought another wave of stress.

The employee names and phone numbers filled three sheets, but it would take Thomas a couple of days to assemble the names and numbers of anyone else who was at the construction site. City employees, inspectors, mail and courier distribution employees, and the suppliers making deliveries were all individuals Thomas would have to track down. Then he'd have to explain why the police needed to speak with them. The worst among them, of course, was his investor.

Thomas reached for his business calendar, and the journal fell open to the day that he learned about the unsuccessful bid on another property. The property was a more suitable location for his planned development, offering both privacy and a unique view of the lake's spectacular view. The property wasn't for sale, but Thomas's lawyer tracked down the owners of the property and made an offer. It took a few bribes to the registration clerk in the land titles office before they obtained the name of the lawyer on record for the numbered company. But even with Thomas' bid fifty percent higher than the appraised market value, the owners turned it down. Word of his interest in a large plot of land in Lake Pines made its way to a real estate agent, and she had contacted Thomas suggested the site next to the marina. He made an offer just as an investor stepped forward with the promise of funding for the project and within a week the deal was closed. The delay that a murder investigation would cause was something he hadn't planned for.

Simon's promise of a speedy investigation did little to calm Thomas' nerves, especially when Simon asked for the keys to the gate. It wasn't until Thomas pulled out the ring of keys from his pocket that he realized his keys were missing. For the last week, Carlos was the first to arrive and was also the last to leave, negating Thomas' need to use his key. It had been at least a week since Thomas remembered unlocking the gate, and he reluctantly admitted that every employee had unrestricted access to the trailer and that he had no idea when they would have gone missing.

Now Thomas wondered if the project was cursed.

The eco-friendly residential complex was a dream of his since he graduated and would have been the first of its kind in the country. The building was to be equipped with solar power, geothermal heating, and a water recycling unit. Similar developments had been up and running successfully in Norway for years and Thomas believed that the natural beauty of Lake Pines would be the perfect backdrop to develop a blueprint for a project that he could then franchise. Now, he wasn't sure it would be worth it.

He flipped the pages to the day he originally contacted the real estate agent and began to record the name of each and every person that he spoke with or had met with regarding the property. Pausing only briefly to call Oliver and ask him to pick up Lucia from school. Oliver was happy to help and went a step further and offered to watch her until dinner when he and Josh could stop by and join them.

Without the necessity to watch the clock, Thomas began to type the particulars for each person who had stepped foot on the property.

He would leave the name of his investor off the list for a few days, hoping it would buy him some additional time. If the investigation could be finished quickly, he could be up and running again and avoid the need for explanation to the people responsible for funding the project.

Convincing them that one murder on a past construction site was difficult enough, explaining a second would end the project along with his career.

CHAPTER 13

The moment she heard the bell ring on the top of the café door, Kerry turned around, stretched her arm, and waved. She grabbed the last free spot at the back of the café, and Lisa found an extra chair in the storage room so three people could sit at the round wooden table intended for two. Simon and Josh wove their way through the crowded café, stopping only long enough to dodge sharp questions about the murder victims with their pro forma answers.

"*There's nothing to worry about.*"

"*Our officers are keeping a special watch on the town.*"

All of the things that police officers were trained to say to make citizens feel safe while not revealing specifics about an investigation.

Dorothy Donovan reached out and grabbed Simon's wrist as he walked by her table. With her free hand shielding the piece of scone she had just popped into her mouth, she pulled him close, "What on earth is happening, Simon?"

The move and question would have seemed rude and out of place if it came from anyone other than the teacher who guided him through the second and third grades. But Simon took the question in stride.

Simon crouched down, meeting Dorothy's eyes straight on, and smiled,

"There's nothing for you to worry about Mrs. Donovan. As scary as it is, you are perfectly safe. I have extra officers on patrol every night."

"Yes. I noticed a police car drive down my street last night at one in the morning," Dorothy said.

Simon grinned, as he imagined his now eighty-two-year-old grade school teacher peering through her floral patterned sheers, "I'm sure you did, Mrs. Donovan."

"You're making me feel old, call me Dorothy for gosh sakes!"

Simon smiled, but the sound of Mrs. Donovan's first name on the edge of his tongue didn't seem right. "If you have any questions, give me a call, but I want you to know that we are doing everything we can to keep you safe."

Dorothy thanked Simon, released his arm, and then returned to the conversation she was having with her friends. By the time Simon maneuvered through the gauntlet of citizens looking for an explanation for the additional police presence in their neighborhoods, Josh was already seated with Kerry.

"Have you ordered lunch yet?" Simon peeled off his coat and hung it over the back of his chair.

"Yes, and I figured neither of you had a chance to eat so I asked Lisa to make you a sandwich," Kerry said.

"I came straight from Thomas' development site," Simon said. "He looked horrible by the time I left, I felt so badly."

"At least it was you delivering the news and not someone he didn't know," Josh said, wishing that he had a chance to give Thomas a heads up about the body on his worksite.

"Too bad your phone was out of range earlier today," Simon said. "I thought maybe you'd want to swing by and see how he was doing. I didn't have enough time to contact you before we rushed out."

Poor cellular reception was the excuse Josh gave Simon, but in fact, Josh was at an appointment with a grief counselor. After Simon spoke with Bethany, his emotional breakdown at the side of the road forced him to face the fact that he was having difficulty dealing with Wayne's death.

Speaking with a grief counselor was something Thomas suggested right after Wayne died, but Josh thought that diving into work and focusing on their family would be enough to help him deal with the pain of losing his brother.

Twenty minutes into his first appointment, Josh realized he wasn't only suppressing the pain of losing his brother but he was conjuring up the ache he experienced when his parents died. Moving into his childhood home, surrounded by so many things reminded Josh of his family.

His memories were mostly good, but inevitably he always came to the same feeling of emptiness when he realized he was alone.

Even with Thomas and Lucia in his life, losing his brother and parents left him with overwhelming feelings of abandonment. This would pass, the grief counselor promised, with time and commitment to his healing.

At the end of his sixty-minute session, he added his name to a grief support group that gathered for weekly meetings. When Josh emerged from the counselor's office, he powered up his phone to tell Thomas about the decision he made to join the grief support group when he saw Simon's text and listened to his message.

He thought back to how difficult it was for Thomas to face a similar situation in Toronto, and how it almost destroyed him. For now, Josh would keep his sessions with the grief counselor private, until he was sure that Thomas would be alright.

"Did you get a chance to speak with Thomas yet?" Kerry asked.

"I called him as soon as I got Simon's text. He's pretty shaken up but he said that he's going to spend the afternoon gathering all of the names and numbers the officers are going to need for their investigation," Josh explained. "He also said that Oliver was kind enough to pick Lucia up from school today and apparently we're joining you for dinner."

"I heard that too," Kerry said. "Maybe for a few hours we can forget about all the bodies that suddenly appeared in Lake Pines."

"Speaking of that," Simon said. "When can you start on the autopsy for David Woodward?"

"As soon as I leave here," Kerry looked at her watch. "I'll be able to complete my report by the end of the day. Assuming I won't have to wait for any long tests."

Lisa interrupted them and placed three plates on the small round table, "I'm sorry it was a little slow today, guys. We've been busy." Lisa glanced around the room.

"Yeah, I noticed that," Kerry said.

Simon and Josh had already bitten into their sandwiches as the aroma of freshly baked bread wafted up around Kerry's nose.

"I think it's a combination of the warmer weather and the buzz in town."

Simon looked up from his lunch, "You mean the bodies? It's caused that much of a stir?"

Lisa nodded, "Kerry's colorful interview she gave to the paper sparked quite the chatter."

"It wasn't an interview," Kerry explained. "Harry caught me off guard, I was walking home from the art exhibition down at the pavilion."

Josh leaned close to Simon, "That's why I suggested Kerry let us handle any comments on investigations in the future."

They all laughed, even Kerry found some levity in her awkwardness with the press.

"As long as you don't hit another reporter, we should be fine," Simon said, joking back to the time when Kerry almost sent Dave Griffins from the Lake Pines Daily News rolling down the muddy embankment when he snuck into a crime scene and prompted a lawsuit against the town.

"Hey, can I ask you guys a question?" Lisa asked, as she grabbed a chair from a nearby table and sat down next to Josh.

"What's the deal with what happened at Belvedere Field?"

"You know we can't talk about that, Lisa," Simon said. "Even with you."

But something in the way Lisa asked, made it seem like it was not just her civic inquisitiveness. It was something deeper, even more personal.

"What is it, Lisa?" Kerry asked.

"I know this is going to sound strange, but my dad had always said something strange was going on with that property," Lisa was now leaning into the table whispering. "He even went to the police."

"When was this?" Simon asked.

"A long time ago," Lisa waved her hand in the air. "I was a little kid. He would bring it up the odd time but my mom would just shush him and tell him to stop stirring up trouble."

"What did she mean by that?" Kerry asked.

Lisa shrugged, "I have no idea, but my dad was adamant about something bad happening there and I just wondered if it had anything to do with what you found?"

"What did the police do when he told them about his suspicions?" Josh asked.

"They told him to go home and leave the police work to the police."

Simon glanced at Josh and they both knew what the other was thinking. The police were closer than they realized to discovering the unmarked graves but missed them because they didn't listen to Lisa's father. Which meant there was a good chance they'd be able to find someone else who knew about the thirty-one bodies buried in Belvedere Field.

CHAPTER 14

Kerry stared past the door that sealed off the small child's remains in the examination room and to the table where David Woodward's body lay. A long, even, deep gash wrapped around the front of his throat, just like the one on Paul Morrow's neck. And just like the wound found on Paul Morrow, the straight line of the cut showed no signs of struggle before his death.

The only difference between the two bodies was that David Woodward had been found shortly after he had been killed. The latest victim had short auburn hair, cut slightly longer than a military buzz cut with the sides tapered up near his temples and with a small flip on the front of his hairline. It was a hairstyle Kerry saw on most athletic men his age and she could see that it suited his face perfectly. Unlike Paul Morrow, David was short. The measurement on the side of the table recorded his height as five foot six but the bulk of his muscles put his weight at one-eighty-two.

Along with tests that confirmed that the same barbiturate was used, the surface of David's skin and hair were coated with the same disinfectant that was used on Paul Morrow's body. And as with the first victim, David's body and clothes were not stained with his blood.

However, the first thing Kerry looked for and found was the chrysanthemum seed under David's fingernail.

The similarities between the two recent murders and the ones that Kaylum Randall was convicted for in 1974 were unsettling. Were they dealing with a copycat killer or was an innocent man behind bars?

Kerry was sitting at her desk when a woman knocked on her door. She was tall, strikingly beautiful, and her speech was lined with a tinge of an Australian accent but her tone was filled with a heavy sadness.

"Excuse me, are you in charge?"

Her deep green eyes were swollen red from several hours of crying. Josh walked in behind her and nodded in Kerry's direction.

Kerry smiled and introduced herself. "How can I help you?"

"My name is Kori Bradford, I... I..." Unable to remain composed, her shoulders shook as her body slumped forward. "I'm sorry. Every time I try to say David's name, I break down."

Kerry guided Kori to a chair, sat beside her, and handed her a tissue from the box on her desk. The thing that struck Kerry was that in addition to Kori's beauty, she was quite a bit older than David. Kori was attractive, fit, and looked young for her age, but nothing could disguise the fifteen-year age gap.

"There's no rule book for how you should be able to react in these situations," Kerry said. "I am so sorry for your loss."

“Thank you,” Kori’s voice trembled with each word. “I wasn’t sure what I should do next. I’ve never been in a situation like this before but the police officer told me that I needed to come here and identify David’s body.”

“I thought I’d accompany Ms. Bradford,” Josh said, making the decision once he heard that both Bethany and the young officer who accompanied her to identify Paul’s body had collapsed when the sheet was pulled back.

Kerry nodded, “Give me a few minutes.”

Moments later, Kerry was folding back the sheet that covered David Woodward’s body. She shielded the wound across David’s throat, folding the sheet under his chin.

Kori nodded, her sobs pushing through her pursed lips and clenched jaw, "That's him."

Josh placed his arm around Kori's shoulder and guided her out of the room while Kerry pulled the sheet over David's head.

In Kerry's office, Kori struggled to compose herself but when she was able to speak she had asked about his personal effects.

"I'm sorry," Kerry apologized. "David was only found with the clothes he was wearing. Did you give a list of what other items he had with him?"

"He would've had his wallet and phone, plus he was wearing a necklace that had a small gold charm on it."

"Are you positive?" Josh asked.

Kori nodded and pulled her phone out of her pocket, "This is what it looks like." She showed Josh and Kerry a recent photograph taken on a Florida beach, his shirt off and the necklace clearly displayed around his tanned neck. "He never took it off. I gave it to him as an engagement gift after he proposed at Christmas."

Josh asked Kori to email the photo to him and once she felt strong enough to stand, he walked her out of Kerry's office and drove her home.

CHAPTER 15

Thomas sat in a chair next to the fireplace and placed a hand on the back of Raven's head. The dog leaned in, resting his head on Thomas' knee, and Thomas responded with a gentle head rub.

He was aware of the ordinary and routine activity taking place around him. The conversation between Oliver and Josh, Lucia setting up a tea party, and even the aromatic scent of rosemary and garlic drifting in from the next room.

He tried to recapture the ease in which he often spent hours with the same people but his mind continued to drift back to the image of the paramedics carrying the black body bag away from the construction site.

His work crew awkwardly watched as the lifeless body of David Woodward was placed into the back of the van and the heavy metal doors slammed shut. Some members of his crew stood motionless, yellow hats still perched on the top of their heads and their hands gripped around shovels. More, however, fidgeted as they grew nervous of the growing number of police officers and flashing lights around them. Their fingers wiggling around their safety hats or their hands shifting from their pockets to the underparts of their arms, no one seemed to know what to do or what to say.

Chief among them was Thomas, except he *needed* to say something. He not only had to explain what was happening, but he wanted to put everyone at ease about what the next week in their lives would possibly be like.

He just didn't want to reveal that it was his experience with a murder investigation, and not leadership prowess, that gave him the knowledge of what was about to happen.

Some of his employees were shocked that the police would want to speak with them about their whereabouts over the last two days and how much access they had to the construction site. Most, however, expected the questions. Either knowledge gained from watching crime shows on television or general information reported in the news.

They did their best to cooperate with the police, stifling their protests about the personal intrusion into their lives. And no one complained, at least not directly to Thomas.

Thomas had given Simon a complete employee list before he left the construction site and he promised to email a list of anyone else who had access to the site. Which spanned months of deliveries, meetings, and inspections. Digging back through his journal and compiling names of companies and individuals who accessed the construction site, even if it was only once, was a grueling task. In the end, a total of fifty-one names were handed over to the police.

However, Thomas excluded the name of his investor from the list, and he hoped that Simon would have a better idea of who the killer was before he needed to hand that information over to the police. Confidence in the project relied on confidence in him, which could affect the money that was invested, whether he liked it or not. And if any of the funding fell through, it would not only signal an end to the project development, it could force him into bankruptcy.

"I was going to take the kids to the park tomorrow," Oliver's voice boomed over the chatter and pulled Thomas away from thinking about what happened earlier that day. "The girls' school is closed for parent-teacher interviews and the weather forecast for the day is exceptional."

"I might as well join you since the construction site will be crawling with cops for the foreseeable future," Thomas said with as much light-heartedness that he could muster. "It'll be good to keep my mind on something else."

"I'm really sorry about that," Simon said. "Hopefully, the forensic team can search the property quickly. Especially with the good weather we've been having."

Thomas lifted his chin and smiled, "Thanks. Somehow I don't think that'll make anyone from my work crew feel better about being questioned about a murder investigation. Carlos had three calls this afternoon from guys that are freaking out."

"I'm afraid a lot of people have grown worried about the bodies that were found," Kerry said. "And I can't say that I blame them."

"I just wish the news about Belvedere Field hadn't gotten out so fast," Simon said. "We're getting several calls from residents demanding answers about what's going on."

Thomas sat forward, "Belvedere Field?"

"Yeah, that's where Paul Morrow and the thirty-one bodies were found," Simon said. "I thought you knew that?"

"I guess I've been so busy with the project development that I didn't realize where the bodies were found."

Kerry steered the conversation away from the murders and brought up the recent art display in the pavilion by the water, hoping to alleviate the tension that was building in the room.

Thomas listened, nodding when it seemed appropriate and commenting when asked a question. But he couldn't help but worry that the property he had tried to recently purchase was also the scene of a murder investigation, and it could bring the police a step closer to his past.

CHAPTER 16

Simon parked in front of the prison as the wind blew a fragrant reminder that spring was arriving in Lake Pines. The warm weather and the impressive columns at the top of the steps leading up to the building gave the day a more significant feel than actually existed.

Since 1974 Kaylum Randall had been layered deep inside the stone and iron structure, surrounded by the constant reminder of his crime. Walls and common areas were unadorned by the familiar comforts of a home but had been where he lived for almost fifty years.

Life in prison was an odd term since anyone incarcerated did anything but live. Survival was the primary focus for anyone residing at this correction facility. *Life* to most people implied celebrating special events and basic daily enjoyment, neither of which Kaylum would experience while serving his sentence.

His file had also revealed that fellow inmates had brought a code of conduct down upon him. Enacting judgment that Kaylum's crimes were more heinous than their own because there was no apparent reason for their cause. None of the women he murdered had caused Kaylum or his family any harm. Random murders of innocent women were recognized as unacceptable among the crowd of gang members, bikers, and one particular murderer-for-hire.

There was an accepted and unwritten rule that retaliation for certain crimes was acceptable. Crimes such as the theft of a stash of drugs, a threat made against a family member, or encroachment onto another gang member's territory warranted violent actions against the offending party, regardless if they were male or female. Once fellow inmates learned that Kaylum Randall's victims had lives that were shockingly similar to their own sisters, mothers, wives, and girlfriends – no effort was made to befriend or protect him.

Kaylum was reminded on several occasions where he stood among the hierarchy of criminals that called the same prison home.

Simon and Josh waited in one of the more private meeting rooms while the guard brought Kaylum Randall up from his cell. Even though they were aware of Kaylum Randall's age, they weren't prepared for the extent of frailty in the old man's body.

Wisps of thinning gray hair, stained yellow from cigarettes, were brushed back over his scalp. His skin was spotted with age, and a scab formed over a cut on the outer edge of his left eyebrow. His left eye brandished a greenish-brown bruise, which was clearly the remnant from a large, dark purple welt.

The battered prisoner, however, retained a disturbing sharpness in his dark eyes.

"What'ya want?" Kaylum asked as the guard locked his arm to the leg of the table. "The guard said you had some questions for me?"

Simon paused before speaking, "We do."

"I'm assuming it's not about my current accommodations," a sneer crossed Kaylum's face and as his mouth parted, he coughed up a stained smile.

"It's about the murders you committed."

"You mean the murders you think I committed," Kaylum snapped.

"We want to know who you spoke with about those murders," Simon said.

Kaylum's brows folded inward, and he fixed his stare directly on Simon. He leaned back against the chair and fell silent.

"You can't tell me in the last forty-eight years that you didn't speak with anyone about what you did?" Simon asked. "We're just looking for a name, that's all."

"I told you I didn't commit those murders."

Simon leaned forward, placing his forearms on the table, and stared directly into Kaylum's eyes, "We both know you're guilty but what we don't know is whether you were working with someone else or spent time bragging about what you had done."

Kaylum's eyes darted from Simon to Josh and then he let out a disturbing laugh, so hard that an uncontrollable cough sputtered out of his throat. The smell of rotted tobacco rushed toward Simon.

"It happened again, didn't it?" Kaylum asked. "That's why you're here."

"We're giving you an opportunity to help us out," Simon said.

"And what will I get? Released?"

"No, but we can have you transferred to a prison where you can spend less time getting assaulted."

"I have a better idea," Kaylum leaned forward, meeting Simon's stare with his. "How about you admit you arrested the wrong man?"

Simon flipped open the file that had remained closed and read the first few lines of the psychiatric assessment that was presented to the judge during Kaylum Randall's trial.

"*Kaylum Randall is capable of the psychopathic behavior that is consistent with traits common to some serial killers. This includes sensation seeking, a lack of remorse or guilt, impulsivity, and the need to be accepted by people who regularly shun him. Kaylum Randall has faced similar problems in his childhood development, never gaining the acceptance or love he craved from his parents."*

Kaylum let out a piercing yell and pounded his free hand on the table. The sound was absorbed by the acoustically tiled walls, preventing a reaction from the guard waiting outside the door.

Neither Simon nor Josh flinched.

"I want to talk to my lawyer!"

Kaylum turned his head and yelled toward the door, "Guard!"

This time the door opened, and the same guard who locked Kaylum's arm to the leg of the table stepped inside.

"I'm ready to go back to my cell."

Simon sat back in his chair, "If you change your mind, have your lawyer give us a call. Putting another psycho behind bars may give you someone you can talk to who won't think you're as deplorable as your fellow convicts apparently do." Simon pointed to the slow healing bruise and cut above Kaylum's left eye.

Kaylum pressed his lips together, shook his head, and pushed back his seat. Words seemed to be on the edge of his lips but he held back his comment as he turned around and walked out the door. They waited until Kaylum had turned the corner at the end of the hall before they left. When Simon and Josh walked out of the prison, the day was still warm and traffic had started to build on the road leading out of town.

Warmer weather and the open water always signaled a return to cottage life. Local residents and out-of-town families made their way to the lakefront and island retreats every Friday. Soon it would be time for Simon and Kerry to revisit the idea of buying a small cabin of their own.

"What now?" Josh asked. "Not that I thought Kaylum would be forthcoming."

"He was more helpful than you think."

"How so?"

"He was just as surprised to hear about the recent murders as he was to see us sitting across from him," Simon opened the door of the police car and paused as he leaned on the roof. "He also flinched when I asked if he had revealed any specifics about the murders."

"You don't think he had an accomplice?"

"Kaylum Randall doesn't have enough morals to want to protect anyone but himself. If he had an accomplice, he would have offered him or her up on a silver platter a long time ago," Simon explained. "No. If the two murders resemble the ones Kaylum Randall was sentenced to life in prison for, it's because he told someone about them, not because he's innocent."

They climbed into the police car and drove back to the station to continue their search for suspects. Finding a connection between Paul Morrow and David Woodward would be the first place they'd begin.

CHAPTER 17

The bones that protruded from the earth were almost completely uncovered. The field was marked with wooden stakes marking the graves that had been concealed for close to fifty years. The test results from the first set of remains were all Kerry had to go on, but judging by the position and state of the subsequent remains that had been unearthed, she knew the results would be the same.

The insights gained from hours above a microscope left Kerry imagining the life of the small child that was buried. The colorful bracelet and the advanced illness were the two factors that remained with her when she left the lab and headed back to the field to supervise the exhumation of the bodies.

A member of the forensic team was removing a layer of dirt from a skull, revealing the small frontal orbit. It was another child.

Kerry referred to the print-out from the ground-penetrating radar machine and made a notation next to the recent body that was uncovered.

"I'll have you work on plot twenty-three," Kerry referenced the individual graves which were acknowledged only by a number, indicating the order in which they were discovered. "That one appears to be an adult. Maybe I'll find something outside of an illness that can point us in the direction of where these bodies came from?"

Simon wasn't able to find any records that Belvedere Field was ever used as a cemetery and rural archives were often difficult to search since most of the information still hadn't been digitized. Information about older communities, death certificates, or census records could only be searched on microfilms, which dramatically slowed their investigation.

Kerry watched as the soil above plot twenty-three was cut away and carefully removed and placed to the side. Each scoop of earth that was removed, was stored adjacent to where each body was found.

The field resembled that of an archeological dig, but the scans from the ground-penetrating radar machine had already revealed the secret concealed under the ground and it was nothing like finding a hidden treasure.

A shadow of anger and worry electrified the air, and Kerry watched as the frayed and decaying canvas on the adult body was removed.

It would take a long time to reveal the identity of the remains, but Kerry had a feeling that the adult male that was buried among the children would give her the answer she needed in her search.

At least, she thought, it was a better place to start.

CHAPTER 18

Three blocks from their homes, the playground was filled with children and parents. Days off from school were usually celebrated by excited children and precisely planned by wise parents.

A delicate balance of entertainment and exhaustion was necessary if the day were to end without tears.

Tire a child out too soon, and a long afternoon nap would wreak havoc at bedtime. Spend too much time with crafts or electronic entertainment, then an excess of energy would build up throughout the day and surface in the form of a tantrum around six o'clock.

Thomas acquiesced to Oliver's experience in matters of child exhaustion techniques, rivaled only by the way he could convince both girls to eat broccoli.

"How are you holding up with all of this murder business creeping onto your construction project?" Oliver asked as the two men sat on a bench as Lucia and Dominque began to dig in the nearby sandbox.

"Okay, I guess. There's nothing I can do about it."

"I guess you're right," Oliver said. "But it has to be affecting you. Especially since you have a hefty number of employees."

"Carlos has been a huge help," Thomas said. "The men and women on my work crew respect him. They see him as a friend more than a boss so he's been soothing any nervousness they're feeling. I also told him to make sure they all get paid while the investigation is going on."

"That's good of you," Oliver waved to a group of parents who walked into the playground and then to Lucia and Dominique, reminding them that he was close by watching them play.

"It's not their fault and the last thing they need to worry about is money. Plus, selfishly I want to make sure they'll still be working for me when I'm ready to start up again. If they jump ship looking for another job then I'm going to have difficulty finishing the project with fewer workers."

"How did your investor take the news of the investigation?" Oliver asked.

"They were good about it," Thomas lied.

"Well, hopefully, this mess will be wrapped up before the storm hits," Oliver said.

"What storm? This spring has been spectacular," Thomas looked around the playground. No one was wearing a jacket and most people, like Thomas, were wearing short sleeves.

"There's a low-pressure system moving up from Colorado and it's supposed to be bringing quite a bit of snow along with colder temperatures."

"Great," Thomas grumbled. He didn't mind the colder temperatures but a large snowfall could push back progress on the development even further.

Just then, Dominque began to squirm, rubbing the back of her hand across her face.

"I think the girls are getting tired," Oliver said getting up from the bench and walking toward the sandbox. "Let's head back to our place and I'll put on some coffee for us while the girls have a snack."

Thomas packed up the girls' toys, shaking the sand loose, and slipped them into the bottom of the stroller as Oliver lowered Dominique into her seat.

"I want a ride too!" Lucia squealed, a broad smile stretched across her tiny face.

"Okay, but you'll have to hold onto Dominque since I won't be able to put her seatbelt across her lap with you inside," Oliver lifted Lucia and lowered her in the seat behind his granddaughter.

They walked out of the schoolyard and up the street trying to figure out when the big storm would hit Lake Pines. The weather, as with most Canadians, consumed broad swaths of conversation during the change of seasons.

Neither Thomas nor Oliver saw the man approaching from the side, and they weren't prepared when he reached into the stroller and grabbed Dominique.

Dominique's cry and Lucia's shriek propelled Thomas after the hooded assailant who was running away with Dominique tightly in his grasp. Thomas spent many hours on the track team in high school but it was the innate jolt of being a frightened parent that gave him the fuel to reach them within seconds.

He thrust out his arm and grabbed the back of the kidnapper's hoodie, choosing not to tackle him for fear of harming Dominique. The smaller man was much stronger than he appeared to be, and he struggled against Thomas' grip almost pulling free, but there was no way that Thomas was going to let go.

The abductor's fist snapped back into Thomas' face sending a dizzying pain through his cheekbone when he reached out to grab Dominique. Still, Thomas' grip held strong.

He reached out again, this time grabbing hold of Dominique's body just as Oliver ran up beside them and held out his arm.

The yell tore through the air as the abductor released his grip on the child and covered his face. He cursed as he stumbled away, picking up speed as he rounded the corner, jumping over a fence and then disappearing between two homes.

Thomas pulled Dominique close to his chest, his heavy breathing mixed with tears as he realized how close they came to having the little girl taken from them.

Oliver reached out and pulled his screaming granddaughter into his arms, and buried his face in her neck. Dropping his shoulders and the can of bear spray to the ground, having just saved everyone from a terrible nightmare.

CHAPTER 19

Kerry burst through the doors of the police station moments after Oliver and Thomas arrived with the girls. She dove toward her father, wrapping her arms around both him and Dominique. Lucia was perched on Josh's lap, her arms wrapped around his neck. Neither child was interested in releasing themselves from their parents' arms.

Thomas was describing the attacker as best as he could.

"Everything happened so quickly," Thomas apologized. "All I could think about was pulling Dominique away from the guy who grabbed her."

"You did the right thing Thomas," Simon squeezed his hand on the top of Thomas' shoulder. "And thank God you were there."

"It was your father-in-law that finally got him to release Dominique," Thomas said and then leaned forward and whispered, "Did you know he has bear spray in the baby stroller?"

"No, but I'm not going to argue about that now."

The police sketch artist turned her electronic tablet around when she had completed her drawing, "Is this what the attacker looked like?"

"I think his hair was a bit longer, but yeah, that's what he looked like," Thomas said. "I'm positive."

Oliver looked at the image and agreed, "But now he has a big red blister on the front of his face."

"Why would someone have tried to grab our daughter?" Kerry asked Simon, her arms tightly wound around her daughter's body.

Simon shrugged his shoulders, "I have no idea. It may not even have been targeted directly at Dominique, we have to consider that."

"What if it's this case we're working on?" Kerry asked. "I shouldn't have spouted off to the reporter about the killer being a sick twisted weakling. Maybe it's retaliation for that."

Simon wasn't convinced, however, the number of hours he dealt with serial killers amounted to zero. He also had to consider the fact that he and Josh had just spoken with Kaylum Randall and that maybe they were getting closer to finding out the truth behind the killings than he realized. Either way, it was a situation that warranted top priority for the entire community.

"I don't think your comment to the reporter would have prompted what happened," Simon calmed Kerry. "I think this attack is unrelated. If anyone would be a target it would be you and me, and that hasn't happened. But I'm going to get this sketch out to every officer who will be on the lookout for him."

Oliver looked at Kerry, who then buried her face into Dominique's hair. She couldn't live with herself if holding back information was the cause of her daughter almost being kidnapped. Even though she swore Oliver to secrecy on the night she was attacked on their driveway, she knew now that she had to tell Simon. Especially since it could affect everyone's safety.

Simon caught the surreptitious glance between his wife and father-in-law, "Do you want to tell me what that was all about?" Simon waved his finger back and forth between them. "I know when you both have that look, and I can tell you're hiding something."

"I didn't think it was worth mentioning when it happened, but now," Kerry's words drifted as she tried to find the right words to begin.

"What wasn't worth mentioning?" Simon stepped forward and pulled Kerry and Oliver to the side of the room.

Josh handed Lucia to Thomas, and then turned to Simon, "I'll take care of sending the sketch out to all the officers on their phones and alert systems. You take care of this."

Josh took the electronic tablet and headed directly to Sally's desk. Simon initiated a red alert the moment he learned that someone tried to grab his daughter, now Sally was just waiting for an official sketch to send out to every officer and to post on their social media accounts. Every parent at the park was already aware of what happened, and the unofficial chain of communication had spread the news to most people in Lake Pines.

Parental information groups, neighborhood watch alert systems, and a slew of other private social media groups were wired into each other and established for just this reason. Thankfully, most of the posts consisted of information about store sales and early registration for extra-curricular activities. This was the first time that many of the groups had used the entwined communication for its intended purpose.

Simon placed both hands on Kerry's shoulder, "Please tell me what happened."

"It was the day after I made that comment to the reporter, but I didn't think it was related."

"What didn't you think was related?"

"Someone grabbed me in our driveway when I came home from work," Kerry said in a voice low enough so only Simon could hear. "My dad burst out of the house and Raven grabbed the attacker's arm and pulled him off me. I wasn't hurt and I thought it was just someone trying to steal my wallet."

"Why didn't you tell me?" The question was directed at Oliver as well. "I had a right to know."

"You were so stressed after locating all of those bodies and I didn't want to give you anything else to worry about," Kerry explained. "But now that someone tried to grab Dominique, I'm not so sure it was my wallet the attacker was after."

Simon wrapped his arms around his wife and daughter, "Don't ever think that I'm too busy."

Simon glanced up at his father-in-law who suddenly looked much older than he had earlier that day. Within the span of a few days, Oliver witnessed an attack on his daughter and the attempted abduction of his grandchild.

"That goes for you too, Oliver. I'm never too busy for either of you."

Tears spilled from Oliver's eyes as he nodded. "We should get Dominique home."

Kerry nodded. "I'm going to take my dad and Dominique home and make sure they're settled before I head back to finish my examination. I'm set up at the hospital now. I needed the extra space for all of the bodies." The words felt more in keeping with a horror film than in the course of her normal examinations. "I'll text you when my dad and Dominique are settled."

"I'll have an officer stationed outside our house, but make sure the doors and windows are locked. And keep Raven close by, that dog is going to get an extra treat tonight when I get home."

As Kerry walked by Thomas, she leaned down and kissed him on the cheek, "I don't know how to thank you, Thomas."

Thomas grabbed Kerry and held her close, "You don't have to. Just stay safe."

Simon walked Kerry to her car and he waited until she turned the corner before he walked back into the station and noticed Thomas was still waiting in the station.

"You don't have to wait around Thomas," Simon said. "You've done all that you can and I'm sure Lucia would rather be at home."

"That's not why I waited," Thomas said. "There's something I haven't told you, and it's a secret that might affect your investigation."

CHAPTER 20

It was just after two o'clock when Simon closed the door to his office and Thomas sat down in a chair across from the desk. Simon's eyes, although focused and serious, were not intimidating in his stare. Simon's approach with everyone he worked with was the same. He was always open and easy to talk to, but the one thing he easily lost patience with was dishonesty.

"Now that we have some privacy, why don't you explain what this secret is that could affect my investigation."

"I'm not sure where to begin," Thomas closed his eyes and shook his head. "I'm afraid is not the first time that I have had a murder investigation associated with one of my construction sites."

Simon sat forward, "Do you want to say that again?"

"It happened seven years ago at a construction project north of Toronto. It was before I started my own property development company and I was doing everything I could to impress the partners at the firm. Which included working double the hours for half the pay," Thomas let out a deep sigh and dropped his shoulders. "I thought I was finally getting noticed for the quality of my work and the ability to run an efficient work crew."

"What changed?"

"Everything that could possibly go wrong with that development did. Final bills for equipment came in higher than the original quotes, faulty supplies were delivered, some items went missing from our site, and a construction company poached a quarter of my crew."

"How does this have anything to do with the murders we're investigating?"

"We were almost done with the interior of the structure when one of the HVAC systems on the roof needed to be replaced. I asked my foreman to supervise the replacement and to make sure that the manufacturer didn't try and install a cheaper unit. That's when it happened."

"What happened?"

"The roof collapsed, killing Gus instantly."

Simon shook his head, "Oh, man. That must have been horrible for everyone. But I still don't see how this relates to the murder investigation?"

"When the police investigated they found the inspection reports were altered, and none of the supports or tressels were to code. Every certificate had my signature on it, but the thing was, I never signed any of them."

"Who would've forged your signature?"

"The only people who would've benefited from saving money on the project were the partners of the firm, but I was never able to prove anything. The police believed the signature on the altered invoices was mine and they wanted to charge me for manslaughter."

"You obviously weren't convicted," Simon said.

"The firm's lawyers eventually got the charges dropped once the family agreed to a financial settlement. The settlement was covered by the company's insurance but the damage to my career had already been done. After I left the firm, no one else was willing to hire me."

"And that's why you started your own company," Simon said, putting the pieces of Simon's career together. "That's horrible but I still don't see how it relates to David Woodward's body being found on your site."

"Do you remember that when I initially planned this project that I bid on two other properties?"

Simon nodded.

"One of those properties was Belvedere Field."

"Really?" Simon's eyes widened. "I didn't know it was for sale. I haven't even been able to find out who owns the property, how did you manage to put in an offer to buy it?"

"I'm not from here so I had never thought that property was a public park, especially since there isn't a sign on the field. My lawyer bribed a clerk at the provincial land titles office to get the name of the owner. Ownership of that property is layered by several numbered companies and it took some work, but we eventually got a contact name for a lawyer. I offered way above market value but the owner turned me down. Not long after, I was referred to a real estate agent who pointed me in the direction of the site we're on now."

Simon folded his arms across his chest, "I can see why you hesitated in telling me."

"I've tried to distance myself from the accusations of murder after Gus died. Considering I can be connected with bribing a city official to get the name of the owner of a property where a recent murder victim was found, it didn't seem like the perfect time to come clean with my past problems. Plus, if my investor was to hear of all of this, they'd certainly pull their money and that would mean I'd lose everything."

"How much of this does Josh know?"

"He knows about the accusations and charges from Toronto, but nothing else."

Simon sat back in his chair, mulling over the information that Thomas had just revealed. He wasn't interested in dealing with the issue of his lawyer bribing a city official and he could see no guilt in making an offer to purchase Belvedere Field. Even though the property turned out to be the location of several remains, there was no way Thomas could have known that. The one thing Thomas did have, was the information that Simon and his team were unable to obtain.

Roadblocks and privacy laws prevented him from peeling back the layers that would disclose the name of the person who owned Belvedere Field.

"You know what I'm going to ask you?" Simon handed Thomas a pen. "I need the name and number of the person you called when you tried to buy Belvedere Field."

CHAPTER 21

Honesty and transparency were essential if Simon was to present a case to the prosecutor that would hold up in court. Because of that, he allowed Thomas to fill Josh in on everything he revealed. Simon didn't want any improprieties to hinder a conviction in their investigation.

Once Thomas had left the station and returned home with Lucia, Simon sat down with Josh and formulated a plan to find out who the owner of Belvedere Field was.

"I called the number Thomas gave me but it just went to voice mail, although, I'm not overly hopeful at getting a callback. Since this is the closest we've come to the owners, I called Peter and I'm having him reverse search the number."

"Any idea how long that will take?"

"Not long. We should have an answer today since he can trace it without a warrant," Simon explained. "I have no idea why we keep hitting roadblocks in finding out who the owner is, but hopefully this is the break we're looking for."

"Any more information on the two murders?"

"Both men were killed by the same person. Kerry's autopsy and examination revealed that both bodies had traces of the same sedatives, their wounds are identical and their bodies were cleaned with the same antiseptic."

"Then there's the matter of the chrysanthemum seed."

"Yes, there's that," Simon pulled a file from the edge of his desk and flipped it open. "I've been over Kaylum Randall's file several times, and those murders are identical to Paul Morrow's and David Woodward's. The only difference is the gender of the victims, Kaylum's victims were all female."

"Did you reach out to the prosecutor or the judge?"

"They both passed away over ten years ago, besides, there was a strict information ban during the trial. None of the particulars about the crime was ever made public. The only fact that was ever reported was that Kaylum Randall was caught, charged, and found guilty."

"So, the only way anyone would have known about how each victim was killed would be if that person was part of the trial or the murder."

"Exactly," Simon slapped his hand on the file in the middle of his desk. "If we didn't have this file or the connection to Kaylum Randall, how would we have approached this investigation?"

"Find a connection between the two victims."

"What do we know about Paul Morrow?" Simon asked.

"He was a delivery driver at Timber Grove Lumber and he seemed to get along with everyone. He lived with his fiancée Bethany Wessex in a small house on the edge of town and was never in trouble with the police."

"And David Woodward was a personal trainer who lived in an apartment off Main Street, had just returned from a month-long vacation in Florida, and outside of a speeding ticket, he had a clean record," Simon said reading from David Woodward's file.

"Did you check to see if Paul Morrow had ever been a client of David's?"

Simon nodded, "There was no mention of him anywhere in any of David's files, and he was extremely organized right down to the name of the person who delivered their groceries."

"Who goes to Florida in the spring?" Josh asked, finding the timing of the vacation odd.

"He and his fiancée were celebrating their engagement and it was the first time they could get away."

A thought occurred to Josh with Simon's last comment, "Do you think there could be a connection because of their engagements?" Josh asked.

"Neither Bethany nor Kori knew each other."

"But that doesn't mean David and Paul didn't know each other," Josh pulled David's file onto his lap and opened it up. "They went to different schools, and they're five years apart in age, so that's not the connection."

"When Kerry and I got married, it was just a quick affair we threw together."

"I remember, you had a backyard wedding. It was nice."

"Yes, but Carly tried to convince us to have a large wedding."

"I remember your sister's wedding. Didn't she do some crazy dance at the beginning of the reception?"

"Yes, and they practiced that for months. What if Paul and David were connected by something related to their wedding planning?"

"I'll call Bethany and see if they had any extra groups or events they were participating in and you call Kori," Josh said.

Both Simon and Josh lowered their heads in concentration as they each made a call to the pair of fiancées about the events leading up to and around their wedding. Both conversations were awkward and painful, dredging up memories of a life that neither woman would experience with the men they loved. However, they learned one key piece of information. Both couples had hired the same photographer for their wedding day.

"They both hired Vicky Chan as their photographer. Why don't I go and speak with her?" Josh said.

"Good idea," Simon pushed his chair back and followed Josh out of his office. "I'll let you know if I get any information from Peter."

For the next while, Simon refocused his attention on his daughter's attempted abduction. No leads or sightings had been received, even though the police spoke with several residents and canvassed every shop in town. By now, almost everyone in town had seen the electronic image of the man who tried to take Dominique.

Sally rushed across the room to where Simon was standing, holding the phone in her outstretched arm, "Simon, one of the officers from the construction site has something they need to tell you, and he said it's important."

"Simon here," Simon walked back to his office and kicked the door closed with his heel, cutting off the echo of the voices of the officers talking in the next room. "What did you find?"

"We have covered the entire property and there is no indication that David Woodward was killed on this property. His body was placed here by the killer, which doesn't make sense since it's not an ideal place to conceal a body."

"Unless the killer wasn't trying to hide it. He may have wanted us to find David's body."

"When we searched the trailer we found a jug of the same disinfectant that Doctor Dearborne said the killer used on the victims. Plus two empty ones in the garbage bin."

Simon let out a slow and steady breath. He was going to have to question Thomas about why the high-powered medical grade disinfectant was doing in his work trailer.

A buzz echoed in Simon's ear as another call came in on his phone, "I have to go. Bring me the report and make sure you seal the evidence properly and record it in the file."

"Already done, sir."

Simon pressed the button and switched the line on the phone and saw Peter's name flash up on the screen.

"What did you find out Peter?"

"I have a name for the owner of Belvedere Field, but you're not going to like it."

CHAPTER 22

Vicky Chan lived in a charming craftsman-style bungalow that sat in the center of a half-acre lot. The home stood out against the neighboring stone houses with its bright blue wide plank siding, and windows and door accented with an even brighter white trim. A hand-painted sign swung from a wrought iron bracket that was nailed on the side of the matching garage that she converted into a studio.

Stylized initials of the local photographer were painted in bright red, and a floral engraving was etched along one side.

When Josh had called, Vicky was preparing her studio for a photo session for a young family. Vicky was arranging a selection of soft toys around the white shag carpet and angling lights against the back screen when Josh knocked on the door.

"Come in," Vicky called from inside her studio. "The door's open."

Josh stepped into the small studio and was amazed at the spaciousness of the converted garage. Extended skylights with louvered screens filtered soft light into the space and softened the appearance of the electronic photo equipment.

"I hope you don't mind," Vicky said as she grabbed a bag of stuffed toys. "I like to prepare for my clients so when they arrive I have time to make them feel relaxed."

Vicky was slender with dark piercing eyes and sleek black hair that slid over her shoulders as she moved. Her voice was soft but strong, and Josh imagined she'd easily put the most nervous child at ease.

"No, that's not a problem," Josh said. "I just have a few questions for you about two clients."

Vicky straightened her back and her smile faded, "David and Paul."

Josh nodded, "I was wondering if you ever had them in your studio at the same time?"

"No," Vicky quickly answered. "They were both just interested in arranging a photo package for their weddings. I always throw in a free engagement photo session for couples that hire me for their big day, but they were never in here at the same time."

"Do you know if David or Paul knew each other?"

"I don't think so," Vicky said. "Sorry, I'm sure that's not what you wanted to hear."

"I'm not sure what I wanted to hear, I was just hoping for some sort of connection."

"I was shocked to hear about their murders," Vicky said and then pointed to the back wall where numerous pictures were stylishly arranged. "They were the nicest guys you could have wanted to meet. All they wanted to do was make their wedding the best day for their fiancées."

Josh stepped toward the wall and glanced at the images. The pictures preserved a happier moment in the young couples' lives, just weeks before their dreams were shattered by the two murders.

Josh took an extra moment to look at the two photos and to try and remember David and Paul how they were when Vicky captured them.

CHAPTER 23

A few hours into interviewing Thomas' employees, it became clear that there was a deep reluctance from a few of the men to reveal their whereabouts during the evening that David Woodward was murdered. After some prompting, Josh learned it had more to do with their spouses learning of their activities rather than hiding information from the police.

After reassurances that he only required the knowledge so they could be ruled out as suspects of a crime, each employee explained where they had been during the hours that David Woodward's body was placed on a pile of soil inside the secure gated area of the construction site. Five were at an all-night poker game, losing enough money that justified their wanting to keep their activities a secret, while two were working a job on the side and were afraid that if Thomas found out that they'd be fired. One was cheating on his spouse and broke down in tears when he admitted what he was doing.

Carlos Davila was the foreman and the final employee to be questioned. Josh had met Carlos several times, but only when he dropped by Thomas' work sites. He didn't know a lot about Carlos, only that he was an employee that Thomas trusted with every facet of his project's operation.

However, as Carlos nervously waited in the chair just outside the interview room, Josh wondered if Thomas' trust was misplaced.

Carlos peeled away the tip of his frayed nail and jumped up from the chair when Josh opened the door and stepped into the hall. The edge of his neck was red, either from a rushed pulse or repeated rubbing with his hand, and Josh had difficulty pulling his eyes away from the deep red marks above his collar.

"Come on in, Carlos," Josh extended his arm toward a chair and Carlos nodded as he walked in and sat down.

"Thanks for coming in," Josh pushed the door closed, and Carlos jumped at the sound. "Is everything alright?"

"Yeah," Carlos waved his hand in the air. "I'm just a little tired."

"I only have a few questions and then you're free to go home."

"Sure, sure," Carlos said. "Anything I can do to help."

"Well, you obviously know why you were asked to come to the station."

Carlos nodded, "The body that the police found."

"Where were you the night before the body was found at the construction site?"

"I was at Phil's," Carlos said. "The bar at the corner of First Street and Willow."

Josh nodded, "I know that place, they used to serve great nachos. Can anyone confirm you were there?"

"Yeah, about four guys. The fifth one passed out at eleven so he won't be too much use."

"I'll want their names," Josh said.

"Yeah, sure, no problem," Carlos fumbled with his phone. He dropped it on the floor before finally picking it up and opening his contact list and reciting the names and numbers of his friends that could provide an alibi for the night David Woodward was killed.

"Do you go to Phil's often?"

"I guess you could say I'm a regular," Carlos said. "I meet the guys there a few times a week. More when there's a game on the sport's channel."

Josh made a note in the file next to Carlos' name.

"Am I in trouble?" Carlos asked.

"Our big concern is figuring out how the murder victim's body was placed inside the locked gate," Josh said. "Thomas said you closed it at the end of every shift."

Carlos pulled both of his hands together and held them on his lap and nodded.

"Did anyone other than you ever lock up?" Josh asked.

"No," Carlos said. "It was my responsibility. I leave after the last employee and I don't return until the next morning."

"Do you have your keys with you?"

Carlos pulled a ring of keys out of his pocket and held them up.

"Are they ever out of your sight?"

"No, never."

Josh folded his hands on the table and lowered his voice, "According to Thomas you were the only other employee who had access to the keys, safe, and trailer on the worksite."

"That's right."

"When Thomas went to give us his set of keys, he didn't have them. He's not sure when they went missing, since you've been locking up and opening for the last couple of weeks."

Carlos' leg bounced against the chair as he slipped his keys back into his pocket.

"Carlos, do you know anything about what happened to Thomas' keys?"

He stared back at Josh, and an awkward silence hung between them until finally, Carlos spoke. "I thought I could get his keys back on his key chain before he noticed but then the cops showed up and we were all escorted off the site before I had a chance."

Carlos dragged his shaking hands across his face and through his hair.

"Last week I lost my keys when I was out watching the game with a few guys and had a few too many beers," Carlos said. "I didn't notice until the next morning that my keys were gone, and when I called the bar they couldn't find them in their lost and found. It was the only place I was, so I knew they had to be there. They must have fallen out of my coat pocket at some point during the night. I slipped Thomas' keys off his ring the next day and had an extra set cut, I just didn't have a chance to put his keys back onto his ring. There always seemed to be someone coming into the office."

"Why didn't you just tell Thomas you lost your keys?"

"He keeps saying how he doesn't know how he'd be able to run the site without me. How would it look if I lost the keys when I was drunk?"

"Do you have both sets of keys with you?"

Carlos pulled the keys out of his pocket again, and this time removed the two keys from his ring and placed them on the table.

"Can you give me a chance to tell Thomas about the keys?" Carlos asked. "It's the least I can do since he put so much trust in me."

Josh put the keys into an envelope and labeled them before placing them in the investigation file. He walked a more relaxed Carlos to the door and wished him luck as he left the station.

He returned to his office and called the bar where Carlos believed he lost his keys.

"Phil's," a woman with a smoke-tinged voice answered the phone.

"Hi, my name's Officer Josh Burgess, I was wondering if you can help me out with something."

"Sure, thing hon," she said. "Anything for Wayne's baby brother."

"Ginny?" Josh suddenly recognized he was speaking with Wayne's first girlfriend. "I didn't know you were still working at Phil's."

"I bought the place when Phil decided it was time for him to retire. I've been running the place for six years now," Ginny said. "How can I help you?"

"Do you have a security camera in the bar?"

"That was one of the first things I installed when I took over. I put a few on the outside of the building and four inside."

"What are the chances you have the recordings from last weekend?"

"Good. I keep them all backed up on my computer, I have recordings that go back six months," Ginny said. "Then I erase them. No point in keeping them if there hasn't been a problem, they take up a lot of memory."

"Carlos Davila was in last week with some friends and he lost his keys while he was there. I was wondering if they were stolen."

"Carlos is a regular fixture here," Ginny said. "I remember him calling frantically looking for his keys but I couldn't find them anywhere."

"Can I come by and look at the video?"

"What's your email?" Ginny asked. "I'll send the recording for the night that

Carlos lost his keys. It'll save you the trip."

Josh gave Ginny his email and after a promise to bring Thomas by for a drink and a plate of her famous nachos he thanked her for her help.

Five minutes later he opened up the file, scanning the video for any sign of the person who may have stolen Carlos' keys.

The image was grainy and the poor lighting inside the bar combined with the greasy film on the camera lens made it hard to distinguish the faces in the recording. Josh fast-forwarded the recording to eight o'clock, just before Carlos said he arrived at the bar. It was a weekday and there weren't many people in the bar. A hockey game was playing on the flat panel television that hung on the wall and everyone's faces were turned toward the screen.

Carlos appeared from the right side of the screen, wearing the same jacket that he had on when he was sitting in Josh's office earlier. He walked directly to a table and after a round of back slaps and handshakes, Carlos waved to Ginny and swirled his hand around the table. Soon Ginny arrived at their table, balancing a tray of drinks, and spent only a few moments speaking with Carlos before leaving to seat the next group of customers.

Most of Carlos' night involved huddled conversations and laughter, speckled with the odd moment of arms shooting up in the air as they cheered on another goal.

It was close to nine-fifteen when Carlos pushed back his chair and walked to the bathroom. A few seconds later the stranger's move had been what Josh was waiting to see. The gesture was subtle and quick, and judging by the number of empty glasses on the table, it was a motion that went undetected by Carlos' friends.

Josh stopped the recording, rewound to the moment just before Carlos left the table, and played it back at a slower speed. Outside of noticing the man push against Carlos' seat, and the slight movement of the jacket hanging on the back of the chair, there was nothing that would've attracted the attention of the men at the table. Josh magnified the view of the recording to get a closer look at the man who had just slipped his hand into Carlos' pocket but his body was turned away from the camera. Keeping his face hidden from view the entire time.

CHAPTER 24

Kerry re-read the report that outlined the forensic team's findings from the excavation. The ground-penetrating radar machine mapped out the entire parcel of land and a total of thirty-one bodies were found. Kerry was looking at a sheet with each grave mapped onto the image of the field, superimposing the hidden horror that lay beneath everyone's feet for almost half a century.

The bodies weren't randomly placed or buried in a large pit, instead, they were lined in the same fashion as if the bodies were intended to be placed at a proper burial site. Except these bodies were not buried in official plots. Belvedere Field had never been a cemetery and not one body was found inside a coffin.

Every single body and every set of remains was placed flat. Their arms were positioned against their sides, and each set of remains was wrapped in a canvas cloth that had mostly disintegrated.

Except for one body that had been disturbed at some point in the last twenty years, the bodies had not been moved since they were placed in the ground. This, the technician was able to distinguish due to the density of the soil that was compacted over the hole that was dug.

It was clear that someone had found one set of remains and instead of reporting it to the police, the body was reburied, packed with soil, and concealed once more.

But why? It was a question that jumped to the front of Kerry's mind, and one she hoped they'd be able to find an answer for.

Hopefully, determining the cause of death would lead to identifying the bodies, and then, in turn, each of them could be given a name.

The first set of remains tested positive for mycobacterium tuberculosis as well as elevated levels of lead. Similar tests were conducted on every set of remains and all of the tests for the children's bones came back with the same results.

Malnutrition, weakened bone structure, and poorly healed injuries were distinguishable on each set of remains. Kerry believed their deaths were ultimately caused by their advanced illness.

Injuries on the ribs of the adult buried among the children stood apart as his cause of death. Small scratches and a gouge that ran along two ribs on the left side of his body pointed toward a stabbing.

Careful notation was made as to the height, gender, and age of the remains. Except for one adult male who Kerry believed was close to fifty-seven, all the other bodies fit the age range of nine through sixteen. Many of the clothes had disintegrated as Kerry had found with the first set of remains she examined. Working slowly, and careful not to damage the material that remained, Kerry measured the waistband, sleeve length, and circumference of the tops to determine the approximate size of each individual.

It would only be an estimate since the level of malnutrition was so great, it was more likely that the bodies were smaller than the size of the clothes indicated.

The final step in Kerry's examination was to scan each skull and generate an image of their faces. DNA samples were extracted from each skeleton and the results would be completed by morning. If any of these children were reported missing, then the facial images and DNA records would help give a name to the unknown victims buried and forgotten in Belvedere Field.

She was unsuccessful in receiving results from her initial submission of the children's dental imprints but held out more hope for the adult male. Both because of his age and the indications of fillings in his teeth.

It was almost eleven o'clock when Kerry had left the hospital and as promised, a police officer was parked outside of their house. He waved to Kerry as she pulled into the driveway and he watched as she made her way safely inside.

The soft yellow glow on the side of the house was gone. Instead, Kerry was greeted by a blinding intensity with the higher-wattage bulb that Simon installed. Every window had been double-checked, every door was given an extra turn of the handle to ensure the new locks were secured, and then a final check was made as Kerry and Simon walked up the stairs and fell into bed.

Soon it would be morning, and most of the world would awaken to a normal start in their day but as Kerry pulled her legs under the covers she knew that everything had changed.

CHAPTER 25

Kerry awoke to the aroma of coffee and cinnamon wafting from the kitchen. Her yawn was the first of the day, but her evening of fitful slumber would make sure it wouldn't be her last.

Every sound, every creak in the floorboards, every shift of the tree branch against the window shutter had jarred Kerry awake. Even Raven sensed the elevated caution and refused to leave Dominique's room, remaining on guard at the base of her crib.

The bedroom door remained open, and Oliver insisted on sleeping in the guest room. The distance between his apartment above the garage and his granddaughter's bedroom was too great he had determined. Little by little everyone eventually relaxed and drifted into a fitful sleep.

Oliver was already in the kitchen pouring his second cup of coffee when Kerry walked down the stairs with Dominique in her arms and Raven following closely behind.

"I can see I'm not the only one who couldn't sleep," Oliver grabbed a cup and filled it for Kerry.

"Simon left forty minutes ago," Kerry lowered Dominique into her high chair and then opened the back door and Raven dashed into the backyard. "I think it's going to take a while before any of us sleep through the night undisturbed."

"I have some pancakes keeping warm in the oven," Oliver handed Kerry the cream from the fridge. "I thought you would need a good breakfast before you head to work."

Kerry leaned over the mug and took a deep breath before she raised it to her lips. "Thanks for this."

"I think I'll stay home today," Oliver said, reading Kerry's mind and answering her question before she had a chance to ask. "Yesterday held a bit too much excitement for everyone."

"By the way, since when have you been carrying bear spray in the baby stroller?" Kerry asked.

"Since the newspaper reported that bears were rummaging through the garbage cans in the neighborhood,"

Oliver explained. “I just never thought I’d use it, especially on a person.”

For the duration of their breakfast, they forced normal conversation with mundane topics as if it would make the horror of what happened the day before miraculously disappear. But the one thing Kerry learned in the course of her job was that nothing ever really went away.

“How are things going with the remains that were found on Belvedere Field?” Oliver asked.

Kerry looked past her father and out into the backyard, “How could so many people be buried without anyone knowing about it?”

Oliver shrugged his shoulders, “There’s always a way if someone wants to keep something hidden.”

"Except for the adult, I think everyone died of tuberculosis or lead poisoning. Or a combination of both."

"And you said you thought they were buried close to forty-five or fifty years ago?"

Kerry nodded. "But that's just an estimate. I sent samples to Toronto for radio-carbon dating, I'll know for certain in a few days."

"Has Belvedere Field always been used as a public park?"

"It's privately owned but Simon said ever since he was a child that it's been used as a public park."

"Has Simon been able to track down the owner?"

"He thinks so," Kerry cut a piece of pancake and popped it into Dominique's mouth. "That's why he went in early.

Peter was able to track down a name from the phone number that Thomas gave him."

"Well, hopefully, it brings you a step closer to getting some answers," Oliver opened the door and Raven bounced into the kitchen and slid three feet into the side of his bowl sending a wave of kibbles over the side and onto the floor. Oliver scooped them up and dropped them back into the dog's bowl, "Any idea who the owner is?"

Kerry shook her head, "Simon didn't want to say anything until he was certain they had the right person. Apparently, it's someone who has made a lot of donations to the town so the implication of a crime isn't one he wants to announce. This family is well-known for their generosity, plus from what I gathered from Simon, that also comes with a flotilla of lawyers."

Kerry downed the rest of her coffee, kissed Dominique, and stood.

"I don't know how late I'll be today, but I'll come home as soon as I'm finished," Kerry promised.

Oliver leaned close and held his daughter's shoulders. "We are all nervous because of what happened, but we'll be safe here. You have a huge job on your plate right now. Let me take care of Dominique and you take care of giving those unknown victims names."

Kerry thanked her father and left, knowing that no matter how hard she tried, a big part of her mind would remain with her daughter.

Kerry arrived at the hospital during the morning shift change and took the back stairway down to the basement to avoid probing questions about the investigation. The hospital basement was now the location for her temporary lab since it was the only secure space she could find to examine such a large number of remains. Her lab was too small, and the local community center was the only other space large enough and was an inappropriate location to bring the bodies.

Most of the tests and examinations had been completed the day before, and she was building her own theory of what she believed happened to the people buried in the field. It was clear that none of the individuals had lived on the property where they found their final resting place.

The property had never been developed and had always been thought to have been a publicly zoned park. In other cases that Kerry could recall, bodies were buried on a property where schools or medical facilities were built. A direct link to the owners of the property could be established and the purpose of the victims being on that land and with those owners was irrefutable. Making it possible to hold someone accountable for the horrors uncovered. However, Belvedere Field didn't give them that luxury. At least not yet.

Care was taken to place the bodies in a grave-like pattern, but the absence of a headstone or marker confirmed that these souls were to remain a secret.

The testing on the clothing, as well as the canvas material that each body was wrapped inside, confirmed the age of the material and could help pinpoint the age of the graves. Kerry requested a broader test on the canvas, knowing that if they were able to trace a large purchase of the material, it could point to where the bodies came from or who buried them in the field.

The emailed report had arrived in her inbox, resting second from the top and marked with a gold star.

The cotton canvas material that was found wrapped around each set of remains had traces of potassium. The DNA sequencing of each of the bodies also was complete, the rush initiated by Kerry was pushed along even faster by Peter's call to the provincial lab. Each of the remains held enough DNA to trace them to living family members, in the event she found some to compare them with. As the reports printed, and the computer scanned, Kerry tried not to imagine the horror of what the mass grave meant.

CHAPTER 26

Prompted by Peter's insistence and reminders of legal issues that arose during previous investigations, Simon spent the first part of his morning speaking with the department's lawyer before calling the man he now believed was the owner of Belvedere Field.

Or more specifically, Simon called the lawyer on record for the man who he believed was the owner of the property.

Cleveland York was the current patriarch of the York family dynasty. Their wealth had been amassed from a variety of businesses, however, the bulk of their estate was established after a string of shrewd property investments during the early days of the building of the railway.

Stretching across the new country and through burgeoning prairie towns, Douglas York's personal connections with a senior railway executive, gave him access to the names of the towns being considered for development.

Hoping to fend off the inevitable land speculation that would take place, the names of multiple towns normally remained classified as the potential sites for future train stations. The final selection was made only after the railway secured the land in the town they planned to build their train depot.

Land speculation was a dangerous business during that time in history but many men believed the potential profit was worth the risk. And Douglas York lived with a streak of daring in every decision he made.

Threats and kidnapping were not unheard of in the days leading up to the announcement of which towns the rail system would be built through. The government believed that keeping the location secret would not only keep the price of land from skyrocketing, but the lack of knowledge in the chosen town or train route could curb the fierce and dangerous competition.

Douglas York, financially backed by his wife's inheritance, purchased several properties in every town that he learned was a potential location for a rail station. After weighing the probable loss in some towns against the potential profit he would garner in other transactions, the young Douglas York set out to register several properties under his name.

He then sold any surplus land to hardworking Europeans who were looking to move to the new country and began a farming enterprise on the prairies. Betting on both sides of the land battle insured Douglas York a winning position.

Never one to lose money, Douglas York eventually grew his wealth and influence in the young country.

Upon completion of the railway, Douglas York settled in Montreal and continued to grow his empire. In addition to the land known as Belvedere Field, York Enterprises retained various properties across the country shielding their ownership in layers of numbered companies and political protection.

"I don't ever remember hearing that the York family had ever established themselves in Lake Pines," Josh read the long list of properties owned by various shell companies under the corporate umbrella of York Enterprises.

"They never did," Simon explained to Josh after he ended his call with the police department's lawyer. "Not one member of the family even had a cottage in the area. The land where the bodies were found happens to be one of many parcels of land that are deemed corporate surplus. The York's have properties like that across the country."

"And why was it called Belvedere Field?" Josh asked.

"Peter believes it was named in honor of one of the mayors of the town after the residents believed he was the one who secured the property. Johnston Belvedere just took the credit and neither he nor his family ever corrected anyone."

Josh returned the file to the top of Simon's desk and leaned back, "How are you going to handle this? I can't imagine it's going to be easy to get a private meeting with Cleveland York."

"I left a message for his lawyer, and considering the property owned by his family's company contains the makings of a concealed cemetery, it'll be in his interest to sort this out before their name hits the news channels along with the story of the bodies buried on the property."

In addition to the York family's political power, they also held the allure of a myth, successfully keeping their photos and names out of the news. Their anonymity was as valuable to the members of the York family as their financial holdings were.

"York Enterprises is privately owned, so they've never had to explain the surplus properties on their books. However, my main concern isn't their ownership of the property, it's the bodies we found buried there."

Josh thought back to the ground-penetrating radar report he read before walking into Simon's office and a chill setting on him again like it did when he first read the print-out. "I read Gavin's report, it was quite disturbing."

"Maybe Cleveland York or his lawyer will be able to explain who dug up the body and reburied it almost twenty years ago."

"I'm afraid at this point it's going to be difficult to shift the blame away from York Enterprises," Josh explained. "Paul Morrow's body might not be attributable to them, but the thirty-one bodies buried for close to fifty years might be."

"There's something else that our investigators found when they were searching Thomas' construction site. I didn't want to say anything until Kerry had an opportunity to test the liquid, but it looks like we found jugs with the same disinfectant on the construction site."

Josh widened his eyes and leaned forward, "Did you tell Thomas yet?"

"I didn't see any point until we had a chance to see if it's even the same product that the killer used," Simon explained. "Plus, so many people had access to the trailer that we will want to look at everyone, not just Thomas."

"I don't know if Thomas is going to be able to handle this," Josh said. "It almost destroyed him when Gus died. He's finally reached a stage in his career where he can really make a name for himself with this project, I'd hate to see him fall back into a slump."

"I don't think that Thomas had anything to do with this," Simon said. "I hope you know that, Josh. I just want to make sure we do everything by the book. The last thing we need is to catch the killer and have them get released on a technicality."

"I think I should give Thomas a heads-up on what you found. If that's alright with you?" Josh asked.

"Sure, I'll leave it up to you to decide how to tell him," Simon said. "Just make sure he doesn't try and go to the construction site. At least until we have a chance to clear everything up."

The phone's blare interrupted Simon and his arm jolted forward as he lifted the receiver to his ear.

His greeting was followed by a woman's voice on the line. "Please hold for Mr. York," the voice was mature, measured, and each word was perfectly annunciated.

There was no polite pause waiting for Simon's response as a hollow click echoed through the line before it was answered by the one person Simon had hoped he would be able to speak with.

"This is Cleveland York," the confident voice was strong but not brash, almost understating the power of the man who spoke into the phone.

"Thank you for getting back to me Mr. York," Simon began. "I have some questions concerning the property you're registered as owning here in Lake Pines."

"Yes, my lawyer told me about the situation. But I don't see what that might have to do with me, Officer Phillips?" Cleveland York was prepared and wasn't going to allow any extension of guilt to reach the shores of his family's investments. "It's quite devastating that all of those bodies were found on the property, but surely you don't think our family had anything to do with that? We have hundreds of parcels of land across the country. They are vacant and unmonitored so there's no way we can be responsible for every person who steps foot on the property."

"That's not what I'm implying, Mr. York," Simon said, knowing he had to tread carefully with each word. "I wanted to know if at any point in time you leased the land to a third party. Did anyone else have access to the land during the years that the bodies were believed to have been buried there?"

"From what my lawyer tells me, the land has been accessed by the public since we tried to sell it in 1920," Cleveland's voice was calm and his words direct. "Between the residents of Lake Pines and the cottagers in the area, a conservative estimation would be that over a million people had access to that property. Not including anyone who may have been traveling through the area."

All of this Simon had already considered.

"No one in our company has ever used that property. We don't have any other holdings in Lake Pines and we don't intend to either."

"Why haven't you sold it?" Simon asked.

"What do you mean?"

"Since 1920, why haven't you sold the property?" Simon asked more specifically. "Land in this region of the country is quite valuable and if the land isn't being used and it's not bringing any money to your company, why haven't you tried to sell it? Someone had to be interested in purchasing the land, it's right on the shoreline and has a unique view of the lake."

"Is owning vacant land illegal, Officer Phillips?"

"No, I'm just curious."

"Consider it one of the many forms of public generosity our company is known for," Cleveland's tone relaxed. "We have many plots of land that are vacant and used by the public. It's one way we give back, I guess."

"That's very generous of your family."

The sarcasm was faint, but it would have been difficult to miss even through the phone line.

"If there isn't anything else, Officer Phillips, I have a meeting in five minutes," Cleveland rushed to end the call.

"Actually there is. I was wondering if I could get all of the financial transactions associated with the property," Simon asked, knowing if he pushed the issue with a judge he'd eventually be able to gather the information. "You know, like tax records, any subdividing or land registrations. It seems as if most of the records are sealed and held under various company names."

"I'll have our lawyer send them to you within a couple of days."

"I appreciate it," Simon said.

After a mumbled response to Simon's acknowledgment of Cleveland York's assistance, the line went dead.

Simon returned the handset of the phone to the base, just as Peter stormed into his office.

CHAPTER 27

There were only a few times that Simon remembered seeing the look of anger mixed with fear in Peter's eyes but none more intense.

"We received this today," Peter held out his arm and Simon grasped the paper in his hand.

Simon's eyes, widened, "Kaylum Randall is trying to get his sentence overturned?"

"He and his lawyer feel that the murders of Paul Morrow and David Woodward hold enough similarities to the murders that he was convicted of, and because of that he thinks his case should either be re-tried or overturned."

"You've got to be kidding!" Simon said.

"And I hate to say it but he's got a pretty good chance to get a new trial."

"How did this happen?"

"After you two left your little meeting with Kaylum, he called his lawyer and had him do some digging," Peter took off his hat and tossed it on Simon's desk as he sat in the chair beside Josh. "No one from the department came to see him since he was sentenced, and he figured it was because there was a similar murder."

"How did his lawyer get information on those murders? We're still investigating them?"

"He claims to have a source in the department."

"You don't sound convinced," Josh asked Peter.

"That's because I'm not," Peter said. "I don't care if Kaylum Randall professed his innocence every day since he was first locked behind bars, I still believe he's guilty."

Both Josh and Simon agreed, there were too many coincidences that Kaylum couldn't explain. If there was any similarity to be drawn between the two timelines it was because Kaylum Randall had something to do with it.

"How long until his lawyer can get in front of a judge?"

"Maybe as early as next week."

"That doesn't give us a lot of time."

"That's why you need to move quickly and find out who committed these two murders. Then we can at least establish why the murderer replicated the murders that Kaylum Randall was sentenced for committing."

Peter looked at Simon and then to Josh and then they all looked to the map of Belvedere Field outlining the graves of the thirty-one bodies found beneath Paul Morrow's body.

"Were you able to speak with Cleveland York's attorney?"

Simon shook his head, "I just finished speaking with the man himself right before you arrived."

"You spoke with Cleveland York directly?" Peter asked. "I was warned that you'd only be able to speak to his lawyer, especially since there weren't any charges against Cleveland or his family."

"And there was something else that was a bit odd," Simon added. "Not illegal, just peculiar."

"Like?"

"Like he never mentioned that Thomas had reached out to purchase the property. Thomas was reluctant at first to tell me about it, but his lawyer and a few strategic bribes were able to get his lawyer's number from the property records. Thomas' offer to purchase was turned down, but it was the lawyer who worked for the York family group of companies that referred him to the real estate agent who eventually ended up brokering a deal for the land he is building on now."

"The site where the second body was found?"

“Exactly,” Simon said. “Don’t you think it’s a little bit of a coincidence?”

“Maybe, but to know for certain, we’ll want to get an identification of where those thirty-one bodies came from and, if possible, who they are.”

Peter made the statement, but it had been on the forefront of everyone’s mind since the discovery of the graves that were furtively concealed in the field. Investigations into missing children filled the news across the country over the last several years.

As each year passed, more stories were shared by families ripped apart by a misplaced view of what was right. Ideals from one group of people layered onto another, their differences giving an impression that one needed to change the other.

But who was responsible for the large number of remains buried in the ground at Belvedere Field?

The answer lay hidden in the identities of those individuals.

This, everyone knew, would be where they would find the answers.

CHAPTER 28

Kerry sat at a table in the back of the café staring at the stack of pages she brought with her from the lab. She chose a seat away from the prying stares of the three women who were sitting near the window, basking in the sun's rays that flooded the front of the café. The warmth from the sun combined with a strong coffee would have given Kerry the fortitude to proceed with reading the over fifty sheets of paper that glared ominously back at her. Instead, she remained distanced from other customers as she shifted her seat at the back of the café and continued to read.

Damage to the remains made examination difficult and direct exposure to the elements for several decades meant that decomposition left little to be tested.

The approximate age of each individual buried in the ground along with the reports that showed signs of tuberculosis and lead poisoning drew a grim picture. Upon the initial discovery in Belvedere Field, everyone believed that the grave was the result of a mass killing, a crime that Kerry would have categorized as deplorable, but one that would have been the result of a single incident.

However, tests that dove deeper into the life of the bones revealed that each person died at a different point in time.

Every death was within close proximity to each other but it was not a mass murder but a more systematic death drawn out over several years. Cruel and painful were two words that came to Kerry's mind.

Before a final conclusion could be made, she wanted to give complete attention to the reports, reading each one with precise attention. Knowing that whatever information she found would become the crux of an investigation.

If her assumption was right, the remains were moved from another location and reburied in Belvedere Field.

Kerry reached into her pocket and pulled out her phone. She dialed Simon's number and waited through four rings until he answered the call.

"What's up, Kerry?" Simon hurriedly answered his phone.

"Is everything alright? Did I catch you at a bad time?"

"Sorry," Simon apologized. "Peter just arrived the moment I got off the phone with the person who owns Belvedere Field."

She sat forward and pressed the phone to her ear, "Who owns it?"

Ownership of the property had remained a mystery since Paul Morrow's body had been discovered.

Everyone was under the impression that the field that bordered the popular forest was owned by the town. However, buried under several numbered companies Simon discovered who owned the property. And with Kerry's recent assumption that the bodies were transferred there from another location, she thought it would finally point to the person responsible for the thirty-one deaths.

"Have you ever heard of York Enterprises?" Simon asked.

"I think I remember a business in Montreal with the name York. But that was a long time ago," Kerry said.

"That's the one."

"From Montreal?" Kerry asked. "Are you certain?"

"Their family and their business go back to the building of the railway. The York family initially made their fortune in land speculation when the railway was being built across the country," Simon explained. "They have properties like Belvedere Field across the country."

"Did he happen to mention knowing who may have been using the field around the time the bodies were buried there?"

"His answer was the same as ours. The public." Simon's deep sigh ended his explanation about the York family's connection to the land. "I hope you're calling with some information we can use."

"Maybe," Kerry whispered into the phone. "I think each person died at a separate point in time."

"It would have been difficult enough to disguise one large burial, are you certain they were buried at separate times?" Simon recalled the precise line and exact measurements between each set of remains. Without land markers or headstones he wasn't sure someone could have managed to bury so many bodies at such precise intervals.

"I said they died at different times, not buried at different times," Kerry clarified. "I want to test some samples from the ground in Belvedere Field. If I can compare samples from inside the graves to other areas on the field I think it would help. If there's a discrepancy in the soil, I can then easily pinpoint the minerals, and then hopefully it can point us toward the location where the bodies were originally buried."

"That's quite a twist."

"That's not all," Kerry tilted her head down at the sheet of paper. "There was one set of remains that was larger than the rest, and I think that person was murdered. There were gouge marks on his ribs which make me think he was stabbed to death. I've run every skull through the facial reconstruction software in my lab and I'll have the results later today. But I have to tell you, Simon, I think whoever that man was and the reason he was killed could also be the reason the bodies were moved."

"I'll have the forensic team collect samples from the field."

"I'd prefer to do it myself," Kerry said. "But have a few people from your team meet me there. I think I'll need the help."

"Alright, I'll text you and let you know when they're on their way."

Lisa was walking toward Kerry, balancing a tray with two cups of coffee and a plate with a warm chocolate croissant as Kerry slipped her phone back into her pocket.

"I thought you could use a bite to eat while you work," Lisa placed the two mugs and the warm pastry on the table and sat across from Kerry.

Although Lisa diverted her eyes away from the pile of paper on the table she knew it had something to do with the bodies found in the field.

"You must feel overwhelmed with everything that's going on," Lisa said. "I was horrified to hear what happened to your dad and Thomas the other day."

Kerry nodded. They still weren't certain what prompted the attempted kidnapping.

"I don't think any of us slept much last night," Kerry reached for her coffee and after she took a drink, she pulled a flaky corner off the warm croissant.

"Do you think the attack had anything to do with the case Simon's working on?"

"Which one?" Kerry had thought the same thing and when she broached the subject with Simon just before they fell asleep, his answer was just that. *Which one*? The idea that any criminal, murderer or otherwise, would cross over into their personal lives brought a deeper level of fear to both of them.

"I hope Dominique is okay."

"Surprisingly she seemed fine, it was the rest of us that were shocked. She's still young enough that I think the entire incident was easy to forget but it might be more difficult for Lucia."

"I'll call Thomas and Josh and see if there's anything I can do for them," Lisa said. “Hopefully all of this can be put behind us sooner than later.”

“Were you ever aware that Belvedere field was privately owned?” Kerry asked. “I’m only asking because I know you grew up here. Neither Simon nor Josh had a clue.”

“No, I always thought that land was owned by the town. Did you learn who the owner was?”

“Have you ever heard of York Enterprises?”

Lisa’s lips pushed flat and the edges of her nose flared out, and she nodded. “My dad worked for them for a brief period. It was always a sore spot in my parent’s marriage.”

Kerry leaned forward, forgetting about her coffee or the warm pastry between them.

"My dad worked for them when he first arrived in Lake Pines. He had been hired as a maintenance worker at a property they owned. He quit after working for them for only a few months and because he was still waiting for his official residency papers, being unemployed would mean he'd have to return to Trinidad."

"What happened?"

"I'm not sure. He was hired by the high school and began to work for them before I was born. But every now and again I'd hear my parents talking about the time he worked for York Enterprises. They'd stop speaking when I'd walk into the room but sometimes I'd overhear part of their conversation and the reason it sticks out in my mind was something my mom always said," Lisa leaned forward and whispered. "She'd tell him that it was a good thing he got out when he did."

"I can see why that would stand out in your memory," Kerry said and then thought of her theory that the thirty-one bodies had been reburied and transported from a different location. "Do you have any idea where your dad worked? There weren't any buildings on the field, so wherever he worked it would have been at a different location."

Lisa shook her head, "He never said. I can see if there's anything at home in his personal papers. There are still a few boxes of his things in the basement."

Kerry's phone buzzed and she removed it from her pocket. The text was from Simon. Two members from the forensic team would meet Kerry at the field in an hour. Kerry thanked Lisa for the coffee and treat, gathered up her papers, and left the café.

CHAPTER 29

Several hours had passed since her conversation with Kerry, but Lisa still couldn't push the memory of her mother's words from her mind. It had been years since both of her parents died and even longer since she thought of the tension and fear that seemed to arise at the mention of her father's first employer in Lake Pines.

She was close to her parents, and as their only child, she was showered with endless streams of attention. The attention that she eschewed throughout her years of adolescence, she now craved to have back in her life. There were never arguments or fights between her parents and the only conversations about their past were interesting or humorous stories of her parents' lives.

Her father's youth in growing up in Trinidad and the carefree life her mother enjoyed being raised in Lake Pines fascinated her. However, Lisa was always more captivated by the story of how her parents met.

The idea of a young woman living in a small northwestern Ontario town meeting the love of her life in an even smaller village on a tropical island was the foundation upon which romance novels were built. And it was part of her family history.

The afternoon crowd had thinned, and only a few tables remained filled with customers. Two with the familiar faces of residents who came to the café every afternoon to eat, drink, and gossip about the lives of people in their neighborhood, and another with a man who was driving through Lake Pines. It was a group that Lisa was confident Candice could handle on her own.

Lisa pulled the string loose from around her waist and tossed her apron, stained with mustard and coffee grinds, into a bin under the counter.

"I'm going to head out early, Candice," Lisa said to the young girl who had become a reliable and capable employee in the short time she worked at the café. "Call me on my cell if you need anything."

Candice waved and continued to work on three lattes ordered by the women sitting at the table next to the window. Candice's work bordered on the conception of art as she created an image of a pine tree in the foam on the surface of their drinks, wiggling the frothy milk back and forth as she poured. Something Lisa always had difficulty in mastering, but Candice did effortlessly.

Lisa had only taken a couple of steps out of the door of her café when the chill in the air wrapped around her body. The balminess of an early spring warmed her when she walked to work that morning, but the weather, like her attention, had shifted.

The recollection of her parents' secret conversations came flooding back with the mention of York Enterprises. Revisiting the moments when she'd hear the relief in her mother's words and knowing she was thankful Lisa's father no longer worked for the same company. It brought back the memory of conversations that Lisa didn't regularly think about.

She pulled the lapels of her light spring coat together and rushed her steps the four blocks home. She lived close enough to the café that she could walk, and just far enough away that if she wasn't dressed appropriately the trip to and from work could be uncomfortable. During the winter months, Lisa was tempted on several mornings to drive to the café, saving herself the bone-chilling dash down the hill. However, she'd only have to worry about her car engine starting at the end of the day, and instead, she'd opt to leave her car in her insulated garage and brave the elements in her knee-length parka and thick mitts.

The early morning warmth had been a welcomed surprise after the lengthy and unusually cold winter they had experienced. Reports of a series of storms rolling into the area were spreading among the patrons at her café over the last few days, however, Lisa brushed them aside and chose to ignore the dire weather prediction. But she was wrong not to listen to Mr. Barney's insistence that she keep her shovel handy.

The sting of the cool breeze swiped across Lisa's face, her eyes watering as her sinus' took the brunt of the dampness. Her fingers fumbled inside her pocket, searching for her keys as she turned the corner at the end of her street. Once inside the house, Lisa turned up the thermostat and put a full kettle on the stovetop as the old furnace creaked and rumbled in the basement just before a puff of warm air escaped from the vents.

Except for retrieving Christmas decorations, Lisa had only gone into the basement to store the boxes with her parents' belongings after they died. There never seemed a reason to go into the basement. However, the noise coming from the furnace meant she'd be forced to take a look around the dark space. Although she didn't know what she should look for, Lisa flicked on the light and walked down the twenty steps into the basement.

It was during her teenage years that Lisa considered the zone on the lower floor of the home her own private solitude. It was where she and her friends could listen to music at an elevated volume and dance wildly to the music videos on television. However, after she returned from college and began working at the café, she didn't have time to hang out with friends as they danced and listened to music. It was a space filled with both pleasant and painful memories, and those two things were irreconcilable. She had been in the basement when a policeman called to let her know that her parents were killed in a car accident, and it was on the pine storage shelves at the back of the basement that boxes of her parents' belongings were stored.

A powerful scent of dust wafted up from the basement when Lisa began to walk down the stairway. The orange and brown shag carpet had never been replaced, and Lisa didn't see the value in renovating the basement if it wasn't being used. The furnace, on the other hand, needed attention.

The furnace room was sparse, two old brooms with ragged bristles leaned against the wall, and an empty shelf where her mother once stored jars of jam and pickled vegetables was covered in a layer of gray dust.

A repetitive pinging sound echoed against the side of the metal furnace, sounding like someone was trying to break free. Although she wasn't familiar with the mechanics of the furnace, the grinding sound of the motor convinced Lisa to call a technician to check it out before it completely died. She didn't want to be faced with a broken-down furnace at the beginning of next winter when a rush of service calls always came the same week that the first flakes of snow coated the ground.

Lisa tried to estimate the cost of the repair bill, thinking back to the last time she had the furnace serviced, but realized it would probably come closer to the price of a new unit.

With no skill to repair the furnace herself, pulled out her phone. She called the first number that was displayed at the top of the internet search page and booked a service appointment with the young woman who answered the phone.

She made a note to let Candice know the date and time of the appointment so that she could cover the afternoon in the café while Lisa ensured an operational furnace was installed in her house.

Lisa was heading back up the stairs when she glanced over at the closet where the boxes containing her parents' remaining possessions were stored. Inside were their childhood photos, souvenirs from family trips, and her father's journals.

Even after her father's death, Lisa respected his privacy and never read his journals. Her conversation with Kerry earlier, however, sparked her interest in the first part of her parents' married life, and soon she was pulling the closet open.

The box containing her father's belongings was on the highest shelf. She reached up, wiggled it off the shelf, and placed it on the floor. Memories flooded back with the rising scent of her father's cologne that saturated the contents of the box.

Lisa pulled one of his journals out of the box and flipped through the pages, reading entries at random and learning a bit more about her father.

The journal entries confirmed that he had a difficult time integrating into a culture so different from the one he was raised in. However, along with frustration and loneliness, most entries revealed his life was filled with contentment and happiness.

Her father recalled numerous moments of joy as he and his new bride began to build a life for themselves in Lake Pines, and he eventually felt more at home in the small Ontario town.

She found the journal covering the years that her father first spent in Lake

Pines, which also coincided with the time he was hired to maintain a small building on a remote property. The entries described a small operation that owned a few properties in the area, not the huge conglomerate that York Enterprises became.

The details of where he worked, what he saw, and why he left filled several pages of the journal. His attempt to explain what he saw to the police was also documented along with the explanation that the young officer gave him for not investigating the complaint. Her father received a not-so-subtle warning that his citizenship application was still in the approval stage and that it would be in his best interest to leave the matter alone and to focus on finding a new job.

Lisa sat back on her heels and closed the journal. She wasn't certain if what was contained in her father's journal could help the investigation, but she knew she wasn't the one to make that decision. Lisa pulled her phone out of her pocket and called Kerry and when the call went to voicemail, she hung up and called the police department and left a message for Simon to return her call.

A screeching sound of the fire alarm resounded through the house and Lisa rushed up the stairs and into the kitchen where the kettle, now boiled dry, had a thick pillow of smoke rising from around the base, setting off the fire alarm in the process.

With her hand wrapped in a towel, Lisa pulled the kettle off the stove, dropped it into the sink, and pushed the kitchen window open. Using the same cloth that was wrapped around her hand, she waved the fresh air around the fire alarm that was mounted on the ceiling until it finally fell silent. Leaving a dull pounding echo pulsating in her ears.

It wasn't until she turned around to open the front door that she saw the man standing behind her. In a swift silent move, he wrapped his arm around her neck, covering her face with a pungent-smelling cloth.

Just before Lisa lost consciousness she realized why she recognized the man. He was the lone patron sitting at her café the entire morning. And it occurred to Lisa that he was also sitting two tables over from where she and Kerry were having a coffee and talking about the murders that captivated the residents of Lake Pines.

CHAPTER 30

Kerry arrived at Belvedere Field at the same moment two women from the forensic team were pulling protective suits over their clothes. One woman threw Kerry a look of concern as she approached the police tape, glancing down at the patches of unearthed ground that dotted the field. The other woman lingered a while longer before she wriggled under the yellow tape, her face changing as she realized what the scene meant.

"I need to have a broad selection of soil if I'm going to compare the contents of the graves to the land around it," Kerry instructed the small team that stood awkwardly on the field. "I know how unsettling this may be for you, but the sooner we can collect the samples, the sooner we can leave."

A look of relief flashed across the faces staring back at her, and she knew that in addition to doing a good job, the team with her would also work quickly.

It took a couple of hours, but Kerry left the field and returned to her lab with a large selection of soil. The tests revealed unique minerals and sediments in the soil and the differences in select samples were obvious.

Traces of red clay brick and potassium were found in the soil where the bodies were buried, which wasn't present in any other location on the field.

It hadn't pointed Kerry to a specific location, but it proved that the individuals buried in Belvedere Field had died elsewhere.

She called Simon and told him about her preliminary findings and promised to forward him the results once every test was complete.

"There was something else too," Kerry said. "I was speaking with Lisa today, and she mentioned something interesting."

"About the case?" Simon asked. "Because I really don't have much time for anything else."

"What happened?"

"Kaylum Randall's lawyer is petitioning for a new trial. He's arguing that the two recent murders prove that his client was innocent all along."

"How much of a chance does he have at getting a new trial?" Kerry asked.

"Pretty good, considering the only people who knew the specifics about the serial killings were the murderer or anyone who was involved with the case and trial."

"Let's hope you can track down the person responsible and refute Kaylum Randall's claim of innocence," Kerry said.

"What was it that Lisa told you," Simon asked, but not with much enthusiasm as he changed the subject.

"Lisa mentioned that her father was hired by York Enterprises as a building maintenance worker when he first came to Lake Pines."

"There's not much to maintain on Belvedere Field," Simon said. "He must have worked somewhere else. Any idea of where?"

"No, but Lisa did say that she believed her dad quit after something terrible happened. He even risked being deported if he didn't find another job."

"I wouldn't be surprised if Cleveland York lied to me," Simon said. "In fact, he made a special point to mention that no one from his company had ever been to Lake Pines."

"And if one of the properties has a red brick building, it could lead you to the location where the bodies were first buried, or where the individuals died," Kerry said.

"I'll call Lisa when I get back to the office, I'm just with the search team where David Morrow's body was found," Simon said.

"Thomas' construction site?"

"Yeah, and they found something that's a bit concerning. Three jugs of what appears to be the same disinfectant that was used on the bodies of Paul Morrow and David Woodward. Two empty jugs were found in the garbage bin and one full one was found in the trailer," Simon explained. "An officer is on his way to your lab with the jugs. If you can check them against the traces you found on the bodies, I'd appreciate it."

"Sure. I'm just working on the final steps in the facial recognition program. Thirty-one remains were a lot to run through the software," Kerry said. "It's going to be a busy week for everyone."

"Tell me about it," Simon said. "Look, I have to go but call me as soon as you get the results from your tests."

An officer arrived with the jugs found at the construction site, and Kerry tested the samples against the traces she found on Paul and David's bodies. The chemical composition was an identical match, however, it was a product that was commonly used to disinfect surfaces and could be easily purchased at many supply stores. Tracking down who purchased the disinfectant may be as close to finding a needle in a haystack as they could be.

Kerry knew that Thomas could never be involved in a crime so heinous, but she worried for her friend who had found himself on the edge of a murder investigation. She called Simon who was still at the construction site to give him the news.

"The chemical composition is a match to what we found on the two murder victims," Kerry said, and then cautioned. "But it's such a common product. Businesses are required to follow strict public health regulations since the Covid outbreak, and the same disinfectant can be found at several stores."

"The killer would have needed a fair amount of the chemical, so I'll focus on the supply companies that sell it. But I'm not going to be able to avoid speaking with Thomas."

"Does he know yet?"

"Josh was going to let him know, but I want to find out who ordered their supplies and then have him go over the inventory to see if any jugs are missing."

“I’m going to focus on the remains, I’ve had some results from the facial recognition program and I’m going to fine-tune them so they can be used to identify the bodies.”

“I’ll give Sally a call and have her put together the files for any missing person reports during the years you think the deaths occurred and I’ll have someone bring them over to your office,” Simon said.

“Okay, thanks.”

Kerry put her phone on the counter and pulled up the images on her computer screen. The faces of thirty-one people stared back at her and she just hoped the resemblances were close enough for someone to recognize.

CHAPTER 31

Thomas lowered the phone, his hand and voice shook as he ended the call with Josh. He looked down at the plate in front of him, the sandwich still uneaten, and pushed it away. His appetite faded as the knot in his stomach tightened with each breath.

Panic engulfed him with the sudden realization that he had no control over what was happening.

He couldn't do what he did last time. Waiting for the police to work things out or hoping that his innocence would be enough to clear his name made him feel helpless.

He hadn't slept through the night since David Woodward's body was found on the construction site and the police finding the disinfectant in the trailer worried him more than he let Josh know.

The presence of the disinfectant was easy enough to explain. Ever since the Covid virus outbreak, businesses were required to ensure that all surfaces were clean and his staff was instructed to wipe down all equipment surfaces before and after each use. The jugs were purchased at the same supply store where he received most of the construction provisions. He gave the name of the supply company to Josh and then promised to forward all purchase invoices from that same company.

He couldn't tell Josh everything he was thinking. Not only did he not want to interfere with a murder investigation, but any shadow of a doubt that shone on him could reflect poorly on Josh.

Thomas decided to call the one person that he knew could defend his innocence. His lawyer answered the call on the first ring, an added benefit in being charged two-fifty an hour for legal services.

Barry Greene was not only one of the top legal minds in the country, he was a childhood friend who defended him against the charges that were laid in the workplace accident that led to Gus' death.

Thomas trusted Barry with every intimate detail of his life. There wasn't a problem or a secret he couldn't tell Barry and on more than one occasion he had made unsurmountable problems disappear.

"Thomas, how are you doing?" Barry boomed into the phone. "You must be getting pretty close to construction on the main building by now."

"Actually, Barry, I've hit a bit of a snag."

"What happened, Thomas?" Barry's jovial tone quickly turned serious. Barry's professionalism always assured Thomas that his friend not only had his back but he was more than capable of handling even the most difficult situations.

Thomas gave Barry a brief rundown of the body found on his construction site and the most recent finding of the chemical disinfectant that was found in his trailer.

"Have you spoken with the police yet?"

"Briefly," Thomas said. "I told Simon about the accusations in Toronto and I have already given them all my employee names and phone numbers."

"Good. From now on don't say anything unless you pass it by me first," Barry said. "Or better yet, refer all questions directly to me."

"I don't know if that will be necessary," Thomas said. "After all, I haven't been accused of anything. It'll just make me look guilty."

"You and I both know how quickly situations like this can balloon into something worse. Even when you're innocent. Let's be smart about how you handle this. Promise?"

"Yes, I promise," Thomas agreed, although he didn't know how he'd explain that decision to Josh. "That's not the reason I called you. I want to know who the owners of Belvedere Field are. I know you had one of your connections in the land titles office find their lawyer's phone number when I first made an offer to purchase the land. I want to know who the actual owner is."

"Why?"

"That's where the first body was found, and since it was their lawyer to referred me to the real estate agent who sold me the property I'm building on now, I'd like to be prepared for whatever connection surfaces," Thomas said. "I don't want to ask Josh, for obvious reasons, and much of what the police are investigating is being kept confidential."

"Let me see what I can find out," Barry said. "I'll call you later."

For the next hour, Thomas busied himself with emails and bringing the accounting files up to date, losing himself in the tediousness of paperwork until he heard the loud buzzing of his phone.

"Barry, what did you find out?"

"Nothing."

"What?"

"You heard me, nada, nothing, zip!" For the first time, Barry actually sounded frustrated. "There was no way I was getting the owner's name out of their lawyer. If you want I'll keep trying, but I don't think it'll make a difference."

"No, don't worry," Thomas said. "I don't think I can afford to have you work on this anymore."

"Consider this one pro-bono," Barry said. "For an old friend."

Thomas thanked Barry and tossed his phone across the desk.

As he looked out the window, a thought occurred to him and he bolted from the house. The idea was crazy, and he may even get a door slammed in his face, but Thomas knew he had to try.

He raced across the lawn, around the hedge, and up the steps to Bill Gibbons' front door.

Thomas' hand shook as he pounded on the door, unsure of how he'd explain the particular situation he was in and wondering if his neighbor would even agree to help him.

Bill pulled the door open, a grim scowl on his face, and yelled, "What in the world is wrong with you? I don't have trouble hearing, one knock would've been fine."

“I need your help?” Thomas blurted out.

Bill leaned out the door and looked beyond Thomas and toward his house, “Is it your daughter?”

Thomas shook his head and waved his hand toward his house, “No, she’s fine. She’s at school right now.”

Bill straightened his body and folded his arms across his chest, “Then what’s with the frantic pounding on my door?”

“I need your advice.”

The edges of Bill’s mouth flattened, as did his shoulders, “Advice? For what?”

“You worked for the city before you retired, right?”

Bill nodded, his brows folding inward, “Yeah, why?”

"I need to know how someone can find out the name of the owner of a property in Lake Pines?"

"By someone, you mean you."

"Yes, and it's so important," Thomas emphasized the word 'so' with folded hands and a tilted head.

"What property were you interested in?"

"Belvedere Field."

Bill's eyes widened, "That's where they found those bodies."

"Exactly, and I need to know who owns that land because I know it's not public property."

"Is this some kind of morbid curiosity that's piqued your interest?"

Thomas dropped his head, let out a sigh, and then raised his face to meet Bill's. Fueled by anxious adrenaline,

Thomas blurted out his explanation, "There was another body found. Except, this time it was found on my construction site. The police think that the two murders are connected and since I made an unsuccessful offer to buy Belvedere Field and the owner's lawyer referred me to the real estate agent who sold me the land I'm building on now, it could make me look guilty. I need to find out who really owns that land so I can make sure my name stays clear."

As Thomas' words tumbled forth a rambling explanation, Bill listened intently, paused, stepped back, and opened his door, "You better come inside."

Once Thomas stepped into the house, Bill closed the door and walked into the living room. He sat down at a desk and told Thomas to sit in the chair next to it.

"I still have my log-in credentials," Bill explained while he typed seven digits into the Lake Pine's administrative system. Thomas noticed a vitality that he hadn't seen before in his neighbor and hoped it would lead to his cooperation. "I've been waiting to see how long it takes my replacement to figure out the security breach she's ignored."

The first two tries returned entries of numbered companies, with a law firm as a contact. The law firm was the same one Thomas had called, and he knew that reaching out to them would lead to another dead end.

"There's one other thing we can try," Bill switched pages and opened up a file that contained information on the repatriation of natural fauna to the shoreline areas in Lake Pines.

"During the 70s there was a real push to protect the wildlife in the region and there was a particular focus on shoreline protection," Bill explained. "Because of that, there were tougher rules put into place that controlled everything from how close you could build to the waterfront to what buildings and septic tanks could be added to existing properties."

"There aren't any buildings on that field."

"In addition to the tougher building rules, owners were given a tax credit if they could prove they were going to preserve the natural environment. To receive that grant, a full application had to be submitted to the town council and then we'd approve the credit before we submitted the documents to the provincial board."

Bill smiled and returned his focus to the computer as he continued his search.

"Why are you helping me?" Thomas asked while Bill searched the computer records.

Bill stopped typing and then turned to face Thomas, "Because even though you and I have had our issues as neighbors, I don't think there's any way that you'd be involved in two murders," Bill said. "I think you're a pretty decent guy, and from what I can tell, you're also a good father."

Bill's words were exactly what Thomas needed to hear, and he thanked him for it.

"Let's see what we can find," Bill returned his fingers to the keyboard and began to type.

Thomas folded his hands together and held his breath as Bill entered the final particulars into the search bar. Soon the property owner's name flashed across the screen. For the first time since anyone tried to search, the name of the person who was the rightful owner of the property was discovered. But instead of a sigh of relief, Thomas gasped and dropped his face into his hands when he realized the owner was also the primary investor for his project on the waterfront.

CHAPTER 32

Bill printed out the information and handed it to Thomas.

"Is this what you were looking for?" Bill asked.

"Yes, but not exactly what I expected to see."

Bill folded his arms, "Do you want to tell me what is really going on?"

"First tell me why you want to help me?" Thomas asked. "This could get you in trouble."

Bill looked down at his feet and fidgeted with his arms before they came to rest upon his lap.

"I've only ever felt useful when I was a town councilor. Ever since I retired, it seems like no one has any use for me," Bill looked out the window into his backyard his eyes falling on the tree fort in the back corner of his yard. "Even my daughter moved to Vancouver to finish school."

At that moment Thomas realized that Bill's unapproachable demeanor had more to do with feeling unwanted and lonely than any anger or hate he felt toward him and Josh.

"Then let people see what kind of guy you are," Thomas said. "If you're always pointing out what city rules someone is breaking then people will avoid you. I've been trying to leave for work early just to avoid you stopping me to tell me my grass is too long, or that my truck is parked too close to your property line."

"Really?"

Thomas nodded.

"Sorry about that," Bill muttered.

"Let's start fresh," Thomas suggested.

"Then let me help you with this," Bill pointed at the computer screen where the name of Thomas' investor was still up on the screen.

"What else can you find on the owner?"

"If they had any other property in the area it will be linked together with this property number. The rules were pretty strict when it came to the environment and the shoreline," Bill explained. "It's just not normally somewhere people will think to look."

The search returned two other properties, one was the land where Thomas was building, and the other was a parcel of land that was on the far edge of town.

"This property is about a fifteen-minute drive northeast from here," Bill printed the information, which filled two extra sheets. "Because this property had a few buildings on it, the owner had to submit paperwork which included the blueprints for the building, the septic field, and the names of anyone associated with the maintenance of the property. I don't know if you're going to be able to reach any of the people on the list, but here it is."

Bill pulled the sheet of paper out of the printer and handed it to Thomas.

"What are you going to do with it?" Bill asked.

"I'm not sure, but I think the first thing I should do is call my lawyer."

CHAPTER 33

Josh knew he should probably extricate himself from the investigation. Not because Thomas was becoming a suspect, but because Josh was in a position where he could easily alter evidence - and that could affect any subsequent trial after the investigation.

Telling Thomas that the disinfectant found in his trailer had matched what was found on the murder victims, put Josh in an awkward position.

The call to the supply store was equally frustrating when he learned that more than a thousand jugs had been sold in the last year. With the strict health regulations that followed virus outbreaks, stores and businesses were fastidious about their disinfectant practices, repeatedly wiping surfaces and their hands. In addition to Thomas' purchases, the long list of customers who purchased the disinfectant would make it impossible to use that as a parameter to search for their killer. The knock on Josh's office door came just as he hung up the phone after speaking with the supply store and he was grateful for the distraction.

"Come in," Josh called out.

The door opened and a young girl walked in, "The lady at the front desk said I could come back. Is this a good time?"

Josh shook the girl's hand and offered her a seat as he closed the door. He recognized her from somewhere, but he couldn't immediately place her face.

"You might not remember me, but I worked with Paul at Timber Mart," the girl fidgeted, trying to find a comfortable position on the chair, before finally linking her fingers together and resting her hands on her lap. "My name's Julie."

The mention of the lumber store prompted Josh's recognition, "That's right. You were stocking some shelves when I came back the second time to speak with the manager."

Julie nodded, "I was listening when you were talking with him. I wasn't trying to eavesdrop, but we were all so confused and scared when we heard that Paul was murdered. I guess I was just trying to figure out if his death had anything to do with the store."

Josh shook his head, "We're still investigating but I don't think Paul's murder is directly related to the store. Hopefully, that will put your mind at ease?"

Julie shrugged her shoulders, "Actually, something the manager said wasn't exactly true. I wasn't going to say anything, but after I spoke with my dad he said I should come in and tell you and that you'd decide if it's relevant."

Josh sat in the chair beside Julie, "That's a wise decision. What is it you wanted to tell me?"

He couldn't imagine what the store manager could have lied about since Josh hadn't received all that much information in the first place.

"Paul was a really easy guy to work with, that part was true. But when he told you that Paul never had any problems with customers, that part wasn't."

This, Josh thought, could be significant in their investigation, "What kind of problems did Paul have?"

"Paul was accused of late deliveries and making mistakes with a few orders," Julie said. "But if any mistakes were made it was by the company and not Paul. He's not responsible for loading the truck and filling the orders, that's all done in the warehouse. Paul just gets the address and drives the order to the location."

"Was this the only instance of complaints against Paul?" Josh wanted to make sure he was painting a fair picture of the murder victim. Friends, family, and coworkers tended to remember people who died in a kinder light than how they lived, and it could be the case with Paul Morrow.

Julie nodded, "Yeah. There was only one company that had a problem with Paul. Which is probably why the manager didn't say anything."

"Was there an argument?" Josh asked.

"A pretty big one too by the sound of it, Paul was flustered when he got back to the store," Julie said. "He was worried that he was going to be fired because of it."

"Do you remember the name of the customer?"

"Yeah, it was that new project over by the marina, the one with the fancy sign."

Julie continued to describe the construction site, but Josh didn't need her to go any further. He knew right away it was Thomas' project.

CHAPTER 34

Kerry rubbed the bridge of her nose and then refocused her eyes on the stack of photos spread out on the table, concentrating on the image of the adult male that was buried among the thirty-one bodies.

The computer-generated image of the adult remains closely resembled Doctor Richard Alpin who had been reported missing by his wife.

Judith Alpin remained at home in British Columbia when her husband began work on a research project in Lake Pines. Every Wednesday and Sunday, sharply at seven o'clock at night, Richard Alpin would call his wife, and it was only after two Wednesdays had passed without hearing from her husband that Judith grew concerned.

However, the police report indicated that the hospital had never heard of Doctor Alpin, and with Lake Pines having such a small medical community, the officer didn't see any need to take Judith Alpin's concerns any further.

A secondary note in the file revealed that the officer in charge believed that Doctor Alpin had used the false excuse of the research project as an opportunity to leave his wife and that he didn't think he had gone missing at all. This theory, however, was never shared with Judith Alpin directly. With no children, Judith Alpin had no additional support in her search for her husband and she died without ever learning what had happened to him.

Judging by the photo in the file, Doctor Alpin was a tall man with thinning hair and brown eyes. His bulk exceeded the suggested healthy weight for a man measuring six-foot-two and he stood with a pronounced curve in his back.

No matter what the original investigating police officer thought, Kerry was certain that Doctor Richard Alpin was most definitely in Lake Pines. His curved spine and the confirmation from the dental records proved that.

Using the records on file with the national medical association, Kerry searched for additional information on Doctor Richard Alpin.

After graduating at the top of his class, Richard Alpin began his professional career at a rural hospital in British Columbia. He treated people who had difficulty traveling and accessing medical facilities, and he moved through the province visiting patients that couldn't travel to see him.

An alarm was raised against the young Doctor Alpin when he performed an appendectomy in a make-shift operating room in the back of an old farmhouse. Without sanitary equipment or facilities, the young girl died two days following the operation after contracting a bacterial infection. The girl's family filed a complaint and after a review by the disciplinary committee, his medical license was revoked.

Kerry sat back after reading the entire file and wondered how a disgraced doctor was found buried next to thirty children. She forwarded Doctor Alpin's information to Simon and asked him to try and track down a living relative while she continued to work on the other remains.

Confirming the adult remains belonged to Doctor Alpin was only one part of the equation. Kerry now believed the answers rested with the bodies of the children. She wondered if his medical training was the reason they died or why they were gathered together in the first place.

Every set of remains held important clues to how a person died, why they died, and what their life was like before death. She just needed to figure out what those clues were pointing toward.

Kerry arranged the printouts of the computer-generated images on the wall. Taping them in a straight line at eye level, and then comparing them with the photos in the missing childrens' reports.

The file was long, longer than Kerry had expected it to be. The faces of exuberant children were out of place with the reality that their bodies ended up in an unmarked grave.

Pictures submitted by desperate family members captured happy moments of their children on the beach, in a park, or during a birthday party. It was difficult to recognize most of the children's faces in the photos since they were images taken while in motion, or with a bright smile on their faces. They weren't captured straight on, where the image would make it easy for the police to search for their child. None of the parents thought to have a picture like that on hand. Who would?

Kerry wondered what picture she would have found among their family photos if Simon had to initiate an emergency search for Dominique. Most pictures captured squished faces, wide grins, and squinting eyes. Dominique was either being licked by Raven or digging in her sandbox. No parent ever thought to have a mugshot version of their child ready in case they were kidnapped.

The panic that would have been felt by each parent was impossible to imagine and even though she couldn't return their children home, Kerry at least hoped she could give the surviving families a chance to find peace and closure by giving them answers.

Kerry paused at the fifth photo in her hand, not because the toothy grin caught her attention, but because the child was wearing the same bracelet she found on the first set of remains she examined.

The similarity was unmistakable. Kerry pulled out the report on the missing child and called Simon and began talking before he had a chance to speak, "Simon, I think I've matched one of the children from the photos!"

"Kerry, I was just about to call you."

"Did you find any information on Doctor Alpin?" she asked.

Finally, Kerry thought, they were starting to get some answers.

“We’ve been instructed to end our investigation into the bodies in Belvedere Field,” Simon said. “Except for Paul Morrow, we’re to turn over everything we have to the province.”

“What?” Kerry yelled. “You’ve got to be kidding me? We finally have some information that can identify the bodies and we’re told to stop!”

“As soon as I began to search for information relating to Doctor Richard Alpin I got a call from Commissioner Roberston, who got a call from someone above him. He wouldn’t say who called him, but he didn’t sound happy about it either.”

“I don’t understand,” Kerry fell back into her chair and dropped the file on her desk.

"Apparently Doctor Alpin's file is to be handled by certain departments and ours isn't one of them," Simon said. "Send me all the information you have on the remains and I'll forward them to Commissioner Robertson. He'll make sure that they get to the right department."

Kerry fell silent and her eyes were unmoved from the child with the colorful bracelet who was staring back at her.

"Did you mention you also had a name for one of the kids?" Simon asked.

Kerry lifted the photo she found inside the missing person report filed by the young boy's mother.

"No," Kerry lied. "I think I was just jumping the gun. I'll send you the files I have."

Kerry ended the call and dropped her phone on her desk.

CHAPTER 35

Peter returned Simon's call moments after he got off the phone with Kerry. Neither of them had expected to be removed from the investigation. But they were. And the directive came with no explanation.

"I was just as surprised as you were," Peter said.

"You must have access to the confidential files," Simon said. "All I was told was that the investigation into what happened in the field was being handled by another department."

"I'm not sure how much I can say," Peter said, apologetically.

"Well, you're going to have to give me something. Because between Kerry and the residents of the town, I'm going to have a difficult time explaining why we aren't investigating what happened to those bodies we found in the field."

The frustration in Simon's voice was clear. They had both encountered political red tape and intrusive egos when they worked on murder investigations. But nothing had ever come close to the secrecy surrounding Belvedere Field.

"I'm as frustrated as you are, Simon."

"Then help me understand why we've been asked to stop? You know Kerry isn't going to drop the investigation, she is determined to give each of those remains an identity."

"When I tried to pull up the classified file, I wasn't able to open any of the information related to that case. What I can tell you is that the information was marked as sensitive and that any unauthorized disclosure of the file would cause serious damage to government security."

"Security? Are you serious?"

"The warning is a pro-forma designation that appears on all classified documents or files with sensitive information," Peter explained. "But I think it sounds more like political interference and I'm concerned that Cleveland York might be behind it."

CHAPTER 36

The bright blue sky had been replaced by a steely gray cover, and the warmth in the air was now filled with an icy chill. The weather was a continual source of conversation in Lake Pines, especially since the area was so deeply affected by harsh storms and rapid shifts in temperature.

The promise of an early spring was fading fast and Kerry was certain she could feel the dampness of an approaching snowstorm. The weather app on her phone predicted a Colorado Low was moving across the area, and with it, the system usually brought plenty of wet snow. Fun for Raven and Dominique, but unwelcome for the investigation.

She turned up the heat in her Jeep as she drove down Main Street and exited onto the road leading out of town. She was taking a chance by driving out to the address listed on the missing person's report, but something told Kerry that if the parents were still alive, they'd be living at the same house. Parents of missing children found it difficult to move away when there was the possibility that their child could return home, no matter how slim the chance.

The bungalow sat at the end of a long unpaved road. The path leading up to the porch curved around two gardens, each one filled with small green shoots peeking out of the ground, beckoning the arrival of new plants. Miniature garden ornaments, some hand-painted by children, dotted the garden and yard. Equally colorful pots lined the porch that wrapped around the front of the house. Toys, some shoes, and three folding lawn chairs were piled next to the front door, waiting for the warmer weather when they could be used. All of this Kerry could see from where she parked the Jeep in the driveway.

The wide expanse of the field stretched beyond the house and disappeared into a dense forest, giving the home a fairy tale backdrop. The trees, some with new buds, others nowhere near bloom, swayed with the wind that picked up from the southwest, and a tumble of branches rolled across the lawn.

Kerry reached over to the passenger seat and grabbed the bag with the small colorful beaded bracelet and stepped out onto the driveway.

An older woman, stout and layered in a multitude of colored sweaters, stepped out of her house to meet Kerry as she walked up the path. A weak smile rested on her round face, and the tops of her cheeks were dotted with faint freckles that matched the rosy pink that faintly tinted her lips.

Kerry introduced herself and asked if she was at the right address. The woman smiled. This time the corner of her mouth stretched and disappeared into a dimple on her cheek, "Yes, I'm Joyce Thibert."

Her eyes moved from Kerry's face to the clear bag in her hand and the smile quickly faded. She stepped forward and without speaking reached for the bag that contained the bracelet she had made with her son Adam. Kerry watched as the woman opened the bag, removed the bracelet, and then held it to her lips. A flood of tears ran down the curves of her face and her shoulders trembled. Kerry stepped forward and wrapped her arms around the woman, lowering her body to embrace her.

Kerry guided Joyce back toward her house and closed the door behind them. The howl of the wind was silenced and the warmth of the house and the smell of simmering stew replaced the dampness outside.

There was no need to ask if she had the right house, or if in fact, the bracelet belonged to her child. Instead, Kerry sat next to Joyce while the old woman crumpled forward. Kerry cried with Joyce, not because she knew Adam, but because she could only imagine what it would be like for Joyce to learn so many years after reporting her son missing, that he was dead. Kerry glanced around the room that was filled with family photos, hand-made crafts, and a mismatched jumble of furniture and pillows. It was a common sight in big families with many children. The surface of the refrigerator was obscured with layers of paper filled with crayon drawings. Some were made years ago by young children, and others were more artistic and creative pointing toward the talent of a mature artist.

This, Kerry knew instinctively, was a happy home.

Joyce dragged the sleeve of her sweater across her cheeks and shook her head, "I prepared myself that Adam might not come back, but seeing his bracelet means that there's no hope that he'll return."

"I'm so sorry," Kerry said.

Then the pleading question came, in both Joyce's words and her eyes. "Where did you find him?"

Kerry knew that she wasn't supposed to have contacted Joyce. The mandate that was given to Simon was clear, the investigation of the remains found in Belvedere Field was to end, and all information was to be relinquished to the province. But this was one of those moments when something bigger was happening, and when Kerry put herself in Joyce's shoes, she knew what she had to say.

"Are you familiar with the plot of land that everyone knows as Belvedere Field?" Kerry asked.

Joyce nodded, "It's that field that's next to the forest at the bend in the river."

"That's the one," Kerry confirmed and then took a deep breath. "The police found several remains in the field when they were investigating another crime. They appear to have been buried decades ago."

"How did you know to come here?" Joyce asked.

"I recognized the bracelet from a photograph that was filed in missing person reports."

"I'm surprised the police kept those reports," Joyce said. "We never thought they took any of us seriously when we said our kids were missing."

"How many other kids were missing?" Kerry asked thinking of the bodies of the thirty children in the field.

"About eleven from our town that I can remember," Joyce stood, walked across the room, and pulled a small birch box off the shelf. "This is a list of the children that were reported missing from several rural communities across western Canada. We went to the police, but no matter how many times we pestered them, nothing was ever done."

"They never searched for the kids?"

Joyce sat back down on the sofa, the weight of her body falling into Kerry, "Oh, they said they did, but days and weeks passed without any news. We searched on our own, but after a while, we were just looking in the same places."

Kerry opened the box and pulled out the folded pages that contained the names of each child, along with their ages, dates they went missing, and what the parents thought they were wearing.

"You probably think we're bad parents for not knowing where our children were," Joyce's eyes were still locked on her son's bracelet.

Kerry rested her hand on Joyce's arm, "No, I don't."

Joyce let an uncomfortable smile briefly cross her lips, but only as an acknowledgment of Kerry's kindness. Then the sadness returned.

"Joyce, was Adam sick before he disappeared?"

The old woman turned to Kerry, "What an odd question to ask, but yes he was."

"Do you know what was wrong with him?"

Joyce shook her head, "No, we had just taken him to a doctor a week before he disappeared, but we never had a chance to learn what was wrong with him."

"And were any of the other children sick too?"

Joyce nodded.

"And do you remember the name of the doctor who examined Adam?"

"I'll never forget him, his name was Doctor Alpin."

CHAPTER 37

Kerry left Joyce Thibert's home wondering what she should do next. She didn't regret going against Simon's instructions, especially since she was now able to link Doctor Alpin directly to one of the missing children.

Kerry convinced Joyce to allow her to draw some blood before she left her home so she could positively identify the remains she believed to be that of her son Adam. Joyce consented to the test, but she knew it wouldn't be necessary because Adam would never have removed his bracelet. The bracelet was his creation and a sense of pride for the young boy who, Kerry had learned, loved to swim, fish, and dreamed of becoming an artist.

Joyce had saved each of Adam's drawings. He had sketched out images capturing the distinctive landscapes in Lake Pines. He imagined building a refuge for injured animals, something Joyce said came naturally to her son who often would wander into the house with an injured bird or a wounded rabbit. Sticks and twigs would be secured to a broken leg or damaged wing, as the animal was nestled safely in a folded towel. Adam would patiently feed drops of sugar water to the birds or a mashed-up mixture of greens to the larger animals and he would nurse them back to health. Sometimes staying up throughout the night to watch over them.

When Adam had grown sick, Joyce did what any other mother would do, she cared for him. When he broke his collarbone, she placed his arm in a sling. And when he tumbled from a cliff and broke his leg, she brought him to a doctor to have it examined and set in a cast. Kerry couldn't be certain that the visit to Doctor Alpin precipitated his disappearance, but she knew it was too much of a coincidence. Whether Doctor Alpin was a willing participant in removing children from their homes, or if he was killed while trying to save them, Kerry may never know. But the connection was irrefutable.

Armed with the knowledge that Adam Thibert had been examined by Doctor Alpin and believing they were both buried in Belvedere Field by the same person, Kerry drove toward the police station. She paused when she passed Joe Black's Coffee Shop and parked her Jeep in front of the café. Before she spoke with Simon, she wanted to see if Lisa recognized Dr. Alpin's name, remembering the conversation they had and Lisa's recognition of York Enterprises.

The small bell rang above the door when Kerry pulled it open and she walked into the crowd waiting at the counter. Chatter echoed in the small space as several people waited for Candice to fill their orders. Kerry looked around the café for Lisa and when she didn't see her, she took her spot at the end of the line and waited for Candice to clear the orders.

Candice smiled when Kerry reached the front of the line, "What can I get you, Kerry? Your regular?"

"Actually, I was hoping to speak with Lisa. Is she here?"

"No, but I wish she was," Candice rested her hands on the counter, thankful for the pause from filling coffee orders. "I was expecting her to come in today, but when I called her at noon, her voicemail box was full."

"That doesn't sound like Lisa."

"It's not, but she's been really busy lately. Maybe she just took some time off and forgot to tell me."

Kerry didn't think that was likely so when she left the café she drove directly to Lisa's house to make sure everything was alright. Falling snow and frozen pellets tapped against the windshield as Kerry turned the corner. The predicted Colorado Low was approaching the region, coating the roads with a frosty film. Kerry hated this weather more than blizzards. At least that kind of snow was easy to shovel and what remained was fun for building forts and snowshoeing.

Kerry parked in front of Lisa's house and ran up the path to the porch, tugging the collar of her jacket around her neck. She knocked on the door and waited a few minutes before trying again.

When there still wasn't an answer, Kerry walked over to the front window and pushed her face against the glass. Light from inside the kitchen illuminated the hall, and as Kerry looked into the house, she noticed the broken lamp on the floor.

Kerry rushed to the door, and this time instead of knocking, she twisted the handle and pushed. The darkened hallway and heavy silence stood in contrast to the yellow glow from the kitchen. In addition to the toppled lamp in the living room, a tea towel had been tossed onto the floor and a burned kettle was thrown sideways into the sink. A cold wind blew through the open kitchen window and a dusty scent emanated from the heat vents below the cabinets. It was clear Lisa wasn't in the house.

Kerry pulled out her phone and called Simon. He picked up on the first ring and as soon as Kerry described the scene in Lisa's house, he told her that he was on his way.

CHAPTER 38

The furnace repairman walked up the path, slowing his gait when he realized an officer, and not the homeowner, was standing at the front door. Confused by the presence of police, the repairman stammered each response to Simon's questions.

"You're not in trouble, Sam, I just need you to tell me when Lisa called your office," Simon repeated the question, trying to figure out when the last time someone may have spoken to Lisa.

"She called yesterday," Sam looked down at the worksheet in his hand. "Around four in the afternoon."

"That was just after Lisa left the café," Kerry said.

"She reported a problem with her furnace and wanted to have it serviced," Sam said. "But that's all I know."

After Sam gave Simon all the information he had on the call from Lisa, Simon joined the other officers who were searching the house.

"Wherever Lisa is, she didn't go willingly," Kerry said.

"Why were you here?" Simon asked Kerry as they walked down the hall to search Lisa's bedroom.

"I went by the café to talk to Lisa, and Candice said she hadn't been able to reach her all day," Kerry walked into

Lisa's bedroom. "I just wanted to make sure she was alright."

"It's a good thing you decided to come by. The sooner we can start looking for her, the better chance we'll have in finding her."

"You don't think the same person who killed Paul and David grabbed her, do you?" The worry and fright were clear in Kerry's tone.

Simon rested his hand on her shoulder, "I don't think so, but I don't want to jump to any conclusions too quickly."

"Down here!" The yell came from the basement. "We found something."

Kerry and Simon dashed down the stairs and found an officer standing next to an open box and a phone lying on the floor.

Simon turned on Lisa's phone and checked her call history. "The last number she called was mine."

Kerry crouched down, and picked up the journal that was on the floor next to the box, "This journal belonged to Lisa's father." Kerry waved the book. "These entries are from the time that her father worked for York Enterprises and in it, her father explains why he quit."

Kerry flipped the pages and a name caught her attention. Doctor Richard Alpin was one of the reasons Lisa's father, Sylvan Joseph, quit his job.

The color faded from Kerry's face, "I think Lisa's disappearance has something to do with the thirty-one bodies we found in Belvedere Field."

CHAPTER 39

Josh stared at the file on his desk wondering how he was going to bring up the latest development in the murder investigation with Thomas. Having recorded Julie's report of Paul's argument with someone at Thomas' work site, he had a duty to investigate the connection. He committed to working on the two murder investigations and approach each clue with an unbiased approach, but he knew if anyone else was working on the case that Thomas's actions would be under deeper scrutiny.

Thomas opened the door after a quick knock and stepped inside, “What’s up? You sounded serious on the phone?”

“Close the door,” Josh then motioned to the seat across from his desk. “I need to speak with you about something that was brought to my attention.”

Thomas closed the door, sat down, and waited for Josh to speak.

“A young girl came in to see me earlier,” Josh said. “It was about Paul Morrow.”

“Isn’t that the name of the first murder victim?” Thomas asked.

“Yeah, and he was also the delivery driver for Timber Mart.”

Thomas immediately recognized the name of the lumber company that he placed several orders with.

Josh continued, "Apparently, Paul had a heated argument after making a delivery at your site and it resulted in a complaint with his boss."

Thomas' eyes widened and he leaned forward, "I don't know what you're implying, but a complaint about a delivery doesn't make anyone guilty of murder."

"No, but we have to investigate everything that happened in Paul's life leading up to his death," Josh explained. "An argument between you and Paul needs to be explained."

Thomas let out a deep breath, shook his head, and leaned back in his seat, "We had three deliveries arrive with items missing. Unfortunately, it's not that uncommon, I had the same issues with other projects. Whenever there's a large order there's always a chance that someone will try and skim a few items off the truck. The price of lumber has gone through the roof, and there have been supply chain disruptions that have made even the most innocuous of items a target."

"Did you suspect Paul of stealing from you?"

"No, that would've been too obvious," Thomas said. "Items were probably removed at the warehouse where the truck is loaded. We've had problems with pieces for our machines, drywall, and support brackets. I've pre-ordered the appliances for the residential units because there's been a ten-month backlog, which has strained my budget. I've had to purchase some supplies months in advance, which is why I'm stressed about getting the project up and running again so I can start to pre-sell some units."

"Can you get me the invoices or reports about the missing supplies so I can add them to the file as an explanation as to why you had an argument with Paul?"

"Sure, but it wasn't me who had the screaming match with Paul. It was Carlos."

CHAPTER 40

The box from Lisa's basement was perched in the middle of Simon's desk. Kerry flipped through the pages of the journal while Simon looked through the other contents of the box, both feeling a disturbing sense of urgency. The abandoned box and phone were clues that Lisa was taken against her will, and the connection between what Sylvan Joseph wrote in his journal and the case they were working on was too huge to ignore.

The entries that Kerry was reading pertained to Sylvan's job at the small private hospital just on the edge of town. The hospital wasn't registered with the province and as far as all official health department records were concerned, the two-story red brick building didn't exist either.

Sylvan Joseph was hired as the sole maintenance employee for the small hospital shortly after he arrived in Lake Pines. He had worked for the small unnamed hospital for two months, along with a staff of nurses hired directly by Doctor Richard Alpin. His responsibilities were limited to the general cleaning inside the building and minor maintenance around the property – and it was while he was working that he witnessed disturbing incidents with patients that he found impossible to forget.

It wasn't a time when employees could question their supervisors, especially if the employee in question hoped to have their citizenship papers approved. Reservations about employers or the work they were doing, were not to be voiced. Doing so could have you fired, or in Sylvan's case, deported.

Eventually, Sylvan's conscience won out and he risked being deported when he quit his job and reported the suspicious behavior to the police. His claims of the questionable treatment of patients at the small hospital were met with doubt and disbelief. The officer who took Sylvan's statement refused to file his complaint and told him to forget about York Enterprises and to look for another job.

With nowhere else to turn, Sylvan gave up. He accepted a maintenance position at the local school but the memory of what he saw and what he thought was happening in the red brick walls of the two-story building never faded. He committed those stories to the pages of the journal along with the names of the nurses and one supervisor who watched over every aspect of the facility.

Kerry wrapped her arms around her body as she read the entries. Children were restrained in their beds, none of them able to leave and no families had ever visited.

Painful screams came from examination rooms, and children's lonely cries drifted out of the windows as Sylvan trimmed the lawn around the building. When he had asked why none of the families had visited, Doctor Alpin said it was to promote calm healing in the patients.

Calm was not the feeling these patients were experiencing and Sylvan, overtaken with sympathy, snuck into the crowded hospital room late at night and consoled the children.

Aged nine years old through late teens, the patients were thankful for a friendly face and they spoke freely with Sylvan. He visited them four more times before he went to the police.

During those visits, Sylvan learned that the patients weren't aware of what illness they were being treated for, even though they were obviously sick. But more concerning was the fact that none of their parents knew where they were. The children were from many different backgrounds and lived in small towns across western Canada.

There were only two things the patients had in common. The first was that they were treated by Doctor Alpin before they found themselves in the hospital, and the second was that not one patient arrived of their own free will.

"There is no record of a hospital, private or otherwise, being registered on that property," Simon said. "If we didn't have Lisa's father's journal we may never have known what happened."

"I hope you're not going to drop the investigation now," Kerry said.

"I don't really have a choice," Simon said. "The case has been taken away from us, I'm going to have to turn all of this evidence over."

"But this obviously has something to do with why Lisa is missing. Plus, what about the families of those kids?" Kerry asked. "They didn't even know they were there. You and I both know it's a really good possibility that those kids were used as medical test subjects because of their tuberculosis."

"That's a huge leap Kerry," Simon said. "I agree both Doctor Alpin and this hospital are suspicious, but until we know for certain, we can't jump to any conclusions."

"But I do know!" Kerry snapped.

Simon's eyes narrowed and he leaned close to Kerry, "What do you mean that you know?"

"I confirmed the identity of one missing child and I saw his mother today," Kerry said. "I was on my way back when I stopped into the café to ask Lisa more about what her father knew when I realized she hadn't been into work."

Simon sighed, "I really wish you hadn't done that."

Just as Kerry was about to defend her actions, Josh walked into Simon's office with a nervous Thomas close behind.

"You're going to want to see what Thomas found," Josh handed a stack of paper to Simon.

"Please tell me you haven't been playing detective like Kerry?" Simon said as he flipped through the sheets of paper, trying to figure out what Thomas had just handed him.

Thomas looked at Kerry and blushed, "Sort of. I think. But I don't really know what Kerry did, so I guess I'm not sure."

Simon dropped his arms to his side, "For crying out loud Thomas, just spit it out."

"Bill helped me find some information on the owners of Belvedere Field," Thomas explained the information printed on the sheets of paper in Simon's hands. "By the way, there are a lot of security leaks in the records department."

"Bill? The neighbor who is always giving you grief? That Bill?"

Thomas nodded, "It was a misunderstanding, we're all okay now."

Simon shook his head, "What am I looking at?"

"The owner of Belvedere Field is York Enterprises," Thomas said.

"That we already know."

"Well, I didn't know that, and if I had known that, I would have told you that Cleveland York is the investor for my building project," Thomas said. "Plus, did you know he also owns two other properties in Lake Pines?"

"Not before today."

"Bill found two properties registered to him. One of them is the one that I'm working on now, which is totally shady since he's also my investor, but that's a different issue. And the other one is some property on the edge of town," Thomas pointed to the sheets in Simon's hands. "There's a map showing all three properties and a list of the maintenance employees that were hired by York Enterprises. There was a requirement for the province to register the names. It was some water or land conservation project that offered tax breaks to property owners. But they had to submit a bunch of information to qualify for the money."

"Shoreline protection," Simon corrected Thomas.

"That was it," Thomas said. "My lawyer didn't want me to show you all of this, because of what happened to me before."

"Well, thanks for giving these to me," Simon picked up his phone and dialed a number.

"Who are you calling?" Kerry asked.

"Well between you and Thomas, I'm going to have some explaining to do and I think I need to reach Peter before this goes much further. One thing is for certain, Cleveland York must be throwing his influence around some top-level positions in the province if the case was suddenly pulled from under our feet. And if this has anything to do with Lisa's disappearance then we need to hang onto all the information we have."

As Simon waited for Peter to answer the line, Sally pushed open the door to his office.

"An officer just arrested a man trying to steal some pain killers from the pharmacy shelf and he matches the description of the man who tried to grab Dominique."

CHAPTER 41

A young man of average height, with light skin, and a scruff of copper hair hanging slightly below his ears nervously fidgeted in his seat in the interrogation room. The most distinguishable feature on his face was the blistering burn from the capsaicin that was sprayed from the bear repellant that Oliver aimed directly at him.

Kerry stood behind the viewing glass while Dominique's suspected abductor waited impatiently in the next room. Simon was on the phone with Peter and decided because of his personal association in the case, that it would be in everyone's best interest if he didn't question the suspect.

No one disagreed.

"Unfortunately for him, it looks like he's allergic to capsaicin," Josh said. "But thankfully the pharmacist recognized the image we distributed and called the police."

"Did he have any identification on him?" Kerry asked.

"No, but we're running his prints through the database," Josh explained. "If he's in our system we'll know shortly."

"Did he say anything when he was arrested?" Kerry asked.

"No, but Simon wants me to question him, so I'm going to head in there now. Both of you stay here," Josh paused and then turned around. "Consider that more than just a friendly request."

The door closed and Thomas folded his arms and looked at Kerry, "I'm not exactly sure what he thought we'd do?"

But given their actions over the last day, Kerry and Thomas knew the warning was justified.

Josh entered the room with another officer, as the man who was the prime suspect in Dominique's attempted kidnapping bounced nervously in a chair.

Josh flipped open a file and clicked his pen, "Do you want to give us your name yet?"

The man folded his arms and pursed his lips.

"Okay, that's a no," Josh wrote something down in the file. "Would you like to explain how you received that burn on the front of your face?"

The man shifted in his seat, but still remained silent.

Josh laid his pen on the table and folded his fingers over the file, "I'm going to take a wild guess that this isn't your first dance with law enforcement. And if that's the case, then you'll be in our system just like every one of our special guests. Plus, you've already been positively identified as the person who tried to abduct a young child, and we have reason to suspect you of two recent murders in Lake Pines. That's a lot to stay quiet about."

The man leaped forward, tugging on the handcuff that secured him to the desk. If not for the restraints, his anger would have propelled him out of the chair.

Josh didn't flinch.

"Did you want to say something?" Josh calmly asked.

"I don't know what you're trying to do, but you're not pinning two murders on me. I didn't kill anyone!"

"But you did try and abduct a small child," Josh said. "I noticed that you didn't deny that charge."

The man sat back in his seat and turned his face toward the floor as the door to the interrogation room opened. An officer handed a file to Josh and then left the room. Josh opened the file and nodded his head.

"Nick Hindley. Twenty-nine and a this is your third arrest but your first visit to Lake Pines," Josh closed the file. "It looks like you made a mark for yourself with three more charges."

"I told you I didn't kill anyone," Nick snapped.

"Then why don't you explain what brought you to Lake Pines."

"I was looking for a job."

"And the burn on your face?"

"Steam from my car radiator blew back into my face."

On the other side of the glass, Thomas and Kerry turned their faces toward each other and they both rolled their eyes.

"Well, you've been positively identified as the man who tried to abduct a child, so that one's going to be hard to avoid."

"I have proof that I only got into town a few days ago," Nick desperately offered a small bit of information. "I have gas receipts to prove it."

"Just before you tried to kidnap that child?"

"I want a deal if I'm going to say anything else."

"What information could you have that would be worth giving you a deal?" Josh asked. "We already have a positive identification from a very reliable witness."

"I don't know what murders you are talking about but I do have some information you'll want to have. But I want some assurance that I'm not going to be charged if I tell you what I know." Nick tugged his arm against the strain of the handcuffs and pulled up his sleeve to rub his skin.

On his forearm was a curved row of bite marks. They were bright red, infected, and were exactly in the spot where Raven pulled the assailant off of Kerry the night she was attacked in her driveway.

Kerry stepped toward the door, twisted the handle, and was partway out the door when Thomas grabbed her arm and pulled her back into the room, "Wait, give Josh a chance."

Kerry reluctantly stepped back into the room and stood beside Thomas as they listened in on the interrogation.

"I'll tell you what," Josh said. "You give me the information and then I'll decide if it's worth a deal. Until then, get comfortable."

CHAPTER 42

No matter what words came out of Nick Hindley's mouth, it was obvious that he knew much more than he was willing to admit. But it was more than that, it also looked like he was terrified to speak.

"Please tell me you're not going to bargain with that man?" Kerry burst out of the viewing room just as Josh walked into the hall. "He attacked me and tried to grab Dominique."

"Kerry, I know that, but if there's a chance he has information about where Lisa is or who committed the two murders, we have to draw it out of him," Josh explained. "He's not going to walk, you can be sure of that."

Kerry and Thomas followed Josh into Simon's office where he was just ending his call with Peter.

"What did you get from him?" Simon asked Josh.

"His name is Nick Hindley, he's twenty-nine, and he's not one of our country's most upstanding citizens. He's not admitting to anything either, no big surprise there."

Simon turned to Thomas, "And you are certain that that's the man who tried to grab Dominique?"

"Positive."

"Okay, let's get him in a line-up and have Thomas and Oliver officially identify him," Simon said. "I don't want any reason for this guy to walk. And let's get Vicky Chan in here as well, she's the only connection we have between Paul Morrow and David Woodward. I want to know if she recognizes him, we need to cover every base."

"There was something else. He said that he has information we'll want."

"Are you serious?" Simon said. "What information could he have?"

"It could be information on where Lisa is or who committed the two murders," Josh said. "Those are the only two cases we're working on."

Simon rubbed his hand over his chin.

"Please tell me you're not considering it?" Kerry pulled Simon's arm, twisting his body around to face hers.

"Kerry, he won't walk but we need to be smart how we approach him," Simon explained. “If he has information on the two murders that means he might also have information on where Lisa is and let’s not forget that finding the murderer will also mean that we can keep Kaylum Randall from trying to get his sentence overturned.”

“What did Peter say about the investigation into the remains we found in Belvedere Field?” Josh asked.

“That news is a little better,” Simon said. “We’re to continue with our investigation. He’s arriving with Commissioner Robertson tomorrow and we’ll all go out to the property where we think this hospital was.”

“Commissioner Robertson is showing up too?” Josh asked.

“They’re not happy about the prospect of a private citizen trying to wield their influence over a murder investigation, so they're going to personally oversee our search of the property," Simon turned to Kerry. "Peter also expressed some interest in speaking directly with Joyce Thibert."

"I'll call her and let her know," Kerry said. "It's just sad that this much notice wasn't given when she first reported her son missing. Then maybe he'd still be alive."

Kerry's comment was followed by silence, everyone in the room having thought the same thing as well.

"Let's call Gavin and get him out there with his ground-penetrating radar machine," Simon said to Josh. "If there's anything to find on that property I don't want to miss it."

"Is there anything we can do until then?" Josh said. "I feel silly just standing around."

Simon grabbed the sheets of paper on his desk, "Peter is going to wait to speak with Cleveland York's lawyer to ask why he left out pertinent information on the properties they owned in Lake Pines. He wants to find something that directly links him to the property we're going to search first thing tomorrow morning"

Simon handed one sheet to Josh and kept the other, "Let's see if we can track down any of the employees listed on these sheets. If we're lucky we may find someone who's still alive and willing to talk."

"And Lisa?" Kerry asked. "Have the police officers found any clues in her house?"

"I'm sorry Kerry," Simon wrapped his arm around his wife. "I have officers working overtime tonight. They're going to search everywhere in town for her. We'll find her."

"I just hope it's not too late."

"We all do."

Soon Josh and Simon were searching the names on the employee register in their database hoping to track down someone they could speak to.

It didn't take long to learn that everyone who worked for York Enterprises was dead.

"Can you cross-reference the names with Nick Hindley's?" Kerry asked.

Simon typed the information into the search engine parameters and failed to come up with a match.

"How about the two victims?" Josh asked.

Again, there was no match.

"Kaylum Randall?" Josh suggested.

This time a match linked him to one employee.

"His mother worked as a supervisor at the facility under her maiden name. Her name is Patricia Gallagher, she died two and a half years after Kaylum went to prison," Simon looked up. The connection to Kaylum Randall came as a surprise to everyone. "Whatever happened to Kaylum Randall's house?"

"Nothing," Josh said. "When his file landed on my desk I noticed that he instructed his lawyer to not dispose of his property after his mother died. There's no mortgage on the house and he had enough money to cover any property taxes. I thought it was strange."

"So we can probably get a search warrant."

Josh smiled and pointed his finger at Simon, "I know exactly what you're thinking. I'll get the paperwork filled out and have one signed before the end of the day. It shouldn't be a problem to speed things along since he's also trying to get his sentence overturned."

Josh ran from the office and Simon grabbed his coat off the back of his chair.

"Where are you going?" Kerry asked.

"Once Josh gets that search warrant, he and I are going to get over there and see if we can find any paper or documents his mother may have left behind," Simon explained. It wouldn't have been something the first set of officers would have been looking for and it could have been easily overlooked."

"Great idea," Kerry headed toward the door and Simon placed his hand on her shoulder.

"Josh and I are going," Simon said. "You and Thomas are not part of the police force, in case you forgot."

"Then what can I do?"

"Identify as many of the remains from Belvedere Field. If my guess is correct, there are going to be more families to call."

CHAPTER 43

Kerry grabbed Kaylum Randall's file from Simon's desk, paused, and then without further hesitation tucked the thick file inside her coat.

"What are you doing?" Thomas whispered.

"We're going to find out how Kaylum Randall connects to the bodies in the field," Kerry walked out of Simon's office, turned around, and then called out to Thomas. "Are you coming?"

Thomas followed Kerry out of the police department as she rushed to her lab just a few blocks away. Following

Kerry's hurried steps, Thomas pivoted his head around, expecting to see an officer chasing them down the street. He was pretty certain that what Kerry had done was illegal, but in reality, Thomas was more afraid of ignoring Kerry than whatever Simon could throw at him.

When Thomas walked into the office he gasped at the images tapped to the wall. Thirty computer-generated faces of children lined the wall, their haunting eyes glaring out into the sterile room. The stacked piles of faded and curled missing person files brought the reality of how many lives they were dealing with crashing down around him.

"You really didn't listen when Simon said you weren't supposed to be looking into the identity of the remains," Thomas said.

"And it's a good thing I didn't because we're right back where we started."

"We?"

"You're here, aren't you?" Kerry asked.

Thomas slipped off his jacket and put it on a hook next to the door, "Where do you want me to start?"

"In addition to trying to match up the photos of missing children, we now know there's probably a connection to Kaylum Randall."

"I don't remember hearing that the bodies found in the field were part of the serial killer investigation?"

"They weren't, but you have to admit, hearing Kaylum Randall's name in association with where we think these bodies came from is too much of a coincidence."

"Do you think he killed them?"

"I'm not sure anymore," Kerry said. "Why don't you see if you have better luck identifying some of the children in the photos and I'll read Kaylum Randall's police file."

"That's a thick file," Thomas said, pointing to the bulky stack of paper in Kerry's hand.

"Only some of the information from Kaylum's case was scanned into the computer. This file will have every bit of information that was collected over the three-year investigation," Kerry placed the file on the desk. "Maybe we'll see something the investigating officers missed."

Thomas got to work comparing the images of the missing children with the computer-generated composites taped to the wall. Thomas was glad for the distraction. Helping identify the remains that were buried in the field, at least made him feel useful and kept his mind off the fact that he was directly connected to Cleveland York, who seemed to be connected to the murders in Lake Pines.

He wasn't certain how the outcome of the investigation would affect his project and Cleveland York's investment, but that was something he wasn't going to try and think about for the next little while.

Kerry busied herself with the excessively thick investigative file on the serial killings that eventually led to Kaylum Randall's arrest.

Three years was a long time for officers to be working on one file. The building frustration was evident in every descriptive entry in the file. As days turned into weeks and then months turned into years, there was a wave of smoldering anger that enveloped every officer that was involved in the case.

The serial killer's final victim was a twenty-nine-year-old girl by the name of Cynthia O'Brien. The only reason that the police looked at Kaylum Randall as a suspect was because of the bar's surveillance recording on the night Cynthia disappeared.

Once the police questioned Kaylum, they realized he couldn't account for his whereabouts on the days the other women were killed. When they searched his home, they found a small greenhouse on the property, along with a selection of seeds and soil that were used to germinate new plants. Kerry focused on the itemization of the contents found in the greenhouse. They were things that at the time would have seemed irrelevant to a murder investigation, but after the thirty-one remains were uncovered in Belvedere Field, Kerry thought they stuck out like a sore thumb.

"How much do you know about gardening?" Kerry asked. Thomas fixed her with an inquisitive stare at the strange question.

"A bit. Why?"

"What's a common ingredient in plant fertilizer?"

"Phosphate, Nitrogen, Potassium," Thomas said as he walked over to Kerry's desk and looked down at her file.

"Exactly," Kerry pointed to the list of items found in Kaylum Randall's greenhouse. "Along with the chrysanthemum seeds look what else the police found?"

"Landscape fabric?"

"It's canvas actually. And look at the photos, it's identical to the canvas that was wrapped around each set of remains before they were buried in Belvedere Field," Kerry said. "It would have been used to cover garden beds and wrap trees before the winter. And since the serial killer never used it on his victims, it wasn't mentioned in the file summary."

Thomas looked at the bottom of the sheet, which was signed by the arresting officer and the lead investigator in the case. "This is something else that no one thought to mention either."

Kerry looked at the signature that was scrawled across the bottom of the sheet and the color drained from her face.

CHAPTER 44

The house on the one-acre property was unmaintained and the ground left fallow. The faded wood siding had fallen loose and several boards dangled from rusty nails that once held them secure. Roof shingles were curled and worn at the edges, welcoming snow and rain into the unprotected building. A panel of glass was missing from a window on the left side of the house, and the word killer was spray-painted in red on the front door. Rotted window sills framed cracked windows that were covered in cobwebs, and trailing weeds had taken over the holes in the roof and spaces in the drain pipes.

If there was ever a time that the house was well cared for or the door required locking, it had long passed.

The house and its state were in perfect keeping with the man that Simon believed Kaylum Randall was. There was no doubt in Simon's mind that the police had captured the right man, no matter how many times Kaylum Randall professed his innocence. The prison was filled with men and women who claimed to have been railroaded and falsely accused of crimes but it didn't make it true. Kaylum Randall blamed pressure from frightened residents for his rushed trial and conviction. However, his accusations rang hollow to anyone who investigated the murders. The police may have only been working off a slim amount of evidence, but the evidence they had pointed directly to Kaylum Randall.

"I hope the place hasn't been ransacked," Josh said as stepped onto the front porch, which was sagging with age and neglect.

"The thought had occurred to me as well," Simon turned the handle and the door swung open into the dark house. "To tell you the truth, I'm surprised this place hasn't been burned to the ground. The anger surrounding this case was fierce."

The stale odor of animal urine and dead mice soured the air and both Josh and Simon buried their noses in their sleeves.

“Why don’t we each take a room. That way we can get through here faster,” Simon said and then headed into the first room on the left, and Josh entered the one across the hall.

Faded family photos, old magazines, and lace table cloths filled the closet in the room Simon searched. Josh had unknowingly entered Kaylum’s room which was filled with books on wood carving and horticulture. Neither of which he seemed to excel at as Josh looked around the room at the misshapen and poorly designed wood sculptures.

“I think I found something,” Simon yelled as he opened the second closet.

Josh rushed into the room and found Simon looking through an old faded storage box that he had placed on the end of a bed. Two more boxes, with the same marking on them, were in the open closet behind him.

"D-R-A," Josh read aloud. "Doctor Richard Alpin?"

"This box contains admission records and building maintenance files," Simon fanned through the pages in his hand. "And I'm willing to bet there's even more incriminating evidence in those boxes."

Josh pulled a file out of the open box on the bed, "This is a contract between York Enterprises to lease the land to Doctor Alpin for the use of a private research facility."

"And then there's this," Simon handed a page to Josh.

As Josh read the sheet his face changed from shock to anger, "If this can be verified then it explains why we were initially pulled off the investigation."

"And there are more sheets with names, ages, and medical records of every patient that went through that facility for the medical trials Doctor Alpin was conducting."

Josh pulled the two boxes out of the closet and placed them on the bed and he and Simon began to search its contents.

"What's this?" Josh pulled a leather journal from the bottom of the box, buried under a stack of financial papers.

After reading the first entry Josh realized he was holding the personal diary of Patricia Gallagher.

Josh flipped through the pages, "She recorded everything that happened at that facility."

"How specific are her entries?"

"Various drug tests were performed on patients who had tested positive for a whole range of diseases. A pharmaceutical company had funded the facility and was responsible for putting Doctor Alpin in charge."

"He would have been easy to convince since he had been stripped of his medical license at that time."

"That's not all, there's even a record of what happened on the day that Doctor Alpin died," Josh said. "There was an argument between him and a teenaged patient who tried to escape when a nurse had walked away from her station. Doctor Alpin had chased him down the hall and caught up to him just in time to block his path to the exit. The patient grabbed a letter opener from the reception desk and used it to fight his way out of the building. Doctor Alpin was stabbed during the scuffle and the patient escaped."

"Did it say what happened to the patient?"

"No, but that's what prompted the facility to be shut down. The pharmaceutical company funding the facility was concerned that the patient could lead the police back to the facility. They ordered the project canceled and the few remaining patients transferred to different facilities around the province under false names."

"I wonder why Patricia Gallagher kept all of this information?"

"Probably to protect herself. She obviously wanted to have something to use if the authorities ever came after her. There's also a map of the property," Josh said. “I wonder if the small cemetery is still there?”

“I don’t think so,” Simon showed Josh another file. “The bodies were moved in 1970, and guess who ordered the move?”

“Well, it wasn’t Doctor Alpin since he was among the bodies found.”

“Patricia Gallagher, Kaylum’s mother.”

“What are the chances that Kaylum helped his mother relocate those remains?”

“Really good,” Simon said. “It may have also been what spurred his bloodthirst. That’s right around the time that the serial killings began.”

“How come none of this was found when the police searched Kaylum Randall’s home when he was arrested?” Josh asked.

"Is mother was alive at the time of his arrest. She easily could have hidden these boxes elsewhere," Simon realized something else. "She maybe didn't even know what a monster her son was. When the police pulled up to the house all those years ago, she may have thought they were there because of what happened at the hospital."

Simon and Josh repacked the contents of the boxes and left the house. They hoped that the information they found would be enough to keep Kaylum Randall behind bars and Simon called Peter to let him know what they had found.

"Peter said he'll pass these boxes onto the prosecutor who's arguing that Kaylum Randall should remain behind bars."

Just as Simon closed the truck to the car, his phone buzzed from inside his pocket.

"Hey, Kerry, we're just on our way back," Simon said before a flurry of words tumbled out of Kerry's mouth.

Among the list of items found at Kaylum's house during his arrest was a large amount of canvas garden tarp, and it confirmed the connection that he and Josh just made after reading the journal. But the name of the arresting officer surprised Simon more. As he hung up the phone and told Josh they both wondered why their boss failed to mention his connection to the case.

CHAPTER 45

By seven o'clock the next morning Simon and Josh were standing at the edge of the property owned by York Enterprises and staring at a two-story red-brick building. The land and building hadn't been used in decades, and the deterioration from the elements was visible from the road.

Gavin had started to scan the ground where they believed patients were originally buried. It was a slow process resulting in a grim reminder of the unpleasantness that transpired on the property.

Peter and Commissioner Roberston were walking toward the building, along with a police officer who was going to film the entire search. Simon and Josh opted to remain behind, feeling their time would be better served in helping Gavin with his search outside the building.

"What did Peter say when you showed him the lease document and the agreement York Enterprises made with the government?" Josh wrapped his hands around the cup of coffee and pulled his shoulders up to his ears.

"He's already started an inquiry into who was involved in the decisions that were made. He knows that information could come out that makes the department look bad, but he doesn't care. He wants to make sure the truth is uncovered and that the victims get some justice. Even though it's most likely that everyone involved is already dead."

"Did you bring up the issue of the signature on the file?" Josh asked.

"Not yet," Simon said. "I wanted to do that face-to-face. After all, it doesn't change the guilt of the man in jail."

A cold wind blew across the field, and a torrent of leaves left behind by the previous season swirled around Simon's body. He looked toward the sky as a helicopter circled the property and then landed near the building, setting down just as Peter and Commissioner Robertson neared the front door.

Simon looked in the direction of the helicopter just as a woman jumped out and walked directly toward Peter with a determined gait.

The woman's eyes met Peter's directly, and she shot out her right hand as she held back her long black hair from her face with the other. As Simon got closer, he noticed her hand wasn't extended as a gesture in greeting but as a means of handing a document to Peter.

The helicopter blades stopped spinning and the deafening noise faded as Peter's voice became audible.

"What do you mean we're being ordered to leave?"

The woman folded her arms across her chest and fixed her deep brown eyes on Peter's, her height making it easy to hold his attention.

"I don't know how I can make it any clearer?" The woman pointed toward Josh and Gavin who were watching them from the far end of the field. "And that includes discontinuing any search on this property, inside or outside of the building."

Peter handed the paper to Commissioner Robertson who called back the men who were preparing to enter the building.

"What's going on?" Simon asked.

"And you are?" the tall woman turned toward Simon and fixed him with the same steely stare that she had held on Peter.

"Simon Phillips, from the Lake Pines Police Department," introducing himself without the pleasantries of a handshake. "And you are?"

"Ada Denmark. I'm one of the lawyers representing York Enterprises. I've been sent to ask you to stop your search. You're trespassing on private property, and unless you have a search warrant you'll have to leave immediately."

"What exactly is Cleveland York trying to hide?"

"Are you accusing Mr. York of a crime Officer Phillips? Because if you are, then you better have some solid evidence to back it up, otherwise you'll also be looking at a lawsuit."

Peter interrupted Ada, hoping to bring calm to the tense confrontation that was quickly brewing, "I think what Officer Phillips is trying to say is that we believe that a crime was committed on the property, not that it was committed by Mr. York. We think there's a connection between thirty-one bodies discovered in a vacant field and this property."

Ada turned to face Peter, "It wouldn't be the first time that a large corporation has been in the crosshairs of the public. If any of York Enterprises' competitors got wind of what you're implying, it will affect their business."

Commissioner Robertson folded the sheet of paper and shoved it into his pocket, "Leave your information with Officer Phillips, he'll contact you later today when we have our warrant. Until then, I'll have a couple of officers stationed at the road, ensuring that nothing is removed from the property until that time."

He pushed between Peter and Ada and headed directly to the car and mumbled a warning under his breath, and then turned around and yelled, "And tell your client that it would be in his best interest if he doesn't try and stop us again."

CHAPTER 46

Simon sat on an old wooden bench in the empty hall outside the judge's chambers, holding Patricia Gallagher's diary journal in his hands. He used the time waiting for Commissioner Robertson to read the journal a second time. The entries in Patricia Gallagher's journal described the transportation of the bodies in enough detail that it would be impossible to not make a connection to the remains they found on Belvedere Field.

What had caught Simon's attention was the swiftness in which Ada Denmark arrived with an order to have him and his search team removed from the property. One thing was becoming increasingly clear, Cleveland York knew more about what happened on those properties than he had initially let Simon believe. Beginning with the fact that he owned properties that were linked with the suspicious deaths and burials of thirty-one bodies.

Peter returned from the cafeteria with two watery, extra-bitter cups of coffee in paper cups.

Simon thanked him, lifted the cup to his lips, and then twisted his face at the first taste, "I'll never get used to this coffee."

Peter took a sip and agreed and then tossed his cup into the trash bin beside his seat.

"Do you have any idea how Cleveland York learned we were heading over to the property near East River Bridge?" Peter asked.

Simon shook his head, "Cleveland York has been more secretive about his connection to Lake Pines than I realized. He could easily have been tracking our movements online or through newspaper articles. What I don't understand is how he could've found out we were at the property at East River Bridge so early this morning. Only a few people at the station knew, and Josh and I left early this morning."

"We may not have had a search warrant, but I did have to get approval from my office to have the ground-penetrating radar machine sent back out here," Peter said. "With only one machine, there's a huge demand for its use. Gavin was on his way to Ottawa when I called him, luckily I was able to convince the police chief to let me keep him here for one more day."

The door to the judge's chambers flew open and Commissioner Robertson rushed out, holding a search warrant in his hand.

"We have until midnight tonight to search the property," Commissioner Robertson said. "Is the search team ready to go?"

"I asked Gavin to stick around Lake Pines while you were meeting with the judge. He's at the station with Josh plotting out the most efficient route to scan the property. It's a large piece of land and it'll take some time to search it properly and we don't want to miss anything in the rush."

"Call Josh and have them meet us at the property at East River Bridge. We can start as soon as they arrive."

"I'll call Ada Denmark and let her know that we have a search warrant and that we'll be there until midnight," Simon pushed open the door and they rushed down the courthouse steps. "If we're lucky we can find what we need before it gets dark."

"I'm more worried about the weather," Peter said as they all looked up at the clouds rolling across the sky which also brought a damp, cool chill to the air.

Josh instructed a crew to collect soil samples while Gavin picked up scanning where he left off when Ada Denmark removed them from the property. Simon joined them once he made a brief call to Ada and then after emailing her a copy of the search warrant he ended the call.

"She mustn't have been too happy with your tone," Josh said as he listened to the last part of Simon's call.

"I'm not really concerned with what Cleveland York's lawyer is feeling right now."

Gavin waved his arm in the air, signaling for Josh and Simon, and they rushed over to where he was standing.

"There aren't any bodies beneath the ground here. Do you want me to search the rest of the property?" Gavin rubbed his hands together and blew warm air into his palms.

"Yeah, focus on the west side of the property." Josh handed him his gloves,

"Take these. You need them more than I do."

"Thanks," Gavin slipped his hands into the gloves and started up the ground-penetrating radar machine again.

Simon left Gavin and Josh in the field and headed into the building where Commissioner Robertson was guiding the search.

"How did the call go with Ada Denmark?" Commissioner Robertson asked.

"She wasn't overly friendly, but she still managed to be cooperative," Simon said and then guided the Commissioner away from the two officers searching the main room in the building. "Can I speak with you about something?"

Commissioner Robertson followed Simon, "What's up?"

"Why didn't you tell me that you were the arresting officer in Kaylum Randall's case?" Simon asked.

"Is it relevant?" the Commissioner asked. "Kaylum Randall was tried and sentenced because he was guilty of those crimes."

"The evidence against him was circumstantial, but once he was arrested, the trial moved pretty quickly," Simon said. "Plus he always claimed that he was framed."

"Are you saying that you think Kaylum Randall is innocent and that I framed him?"

"No, but if he's successful in having his case retried because of the similarity of the two recent murders, then those accusations can be used against us. I just want to know if there's anything else I need to be prepared for?"

"I can assure you that the right man is behind bars," Commissioner Roberston said. "And I'll go to my grave to fight that."

Commissioner Robertson turned around and stomped out of the building, leaving Simon standing in the hall. Simon walked outside and saw the Commissioner pull out his phone and stab at the screen, and after an intense glance in Simon's direction, he climbed into his car and left. Simon shook off the interaction with the commissioner and walked over to where Josh was standing, "How's it going out here?"

"Slow," Josh said. "How about inside?"

Simon shook his head, "There doesn't even seem to be a scrap of paper in the building. Everything has been cleared out."

"Found something," Gavin yelled from the far end of the field.

Simon rushed over to where Gavin was standing, his machine paused over a patch of ground near the perimeter of the field. The lawn had been untended and weeds had replaced much of the grass that had stretched around the building. The faint depression in the ground beneath where Gavin was searching was possibly the location of a large garden. The telltale signs of the uneven earth and wilted stems from wildflowers that had faded from the previous growing season dotted the muddied earth. Indications of where the bodies were originally buried appeared as shadows on the screen. But a darker image also appeared and after the soil was removed from the ground, they found a steel box. Inside was Doctor Alpin's research plan along with the names of the government officials that approved the secretive medical testing that was funded by a Pharmacy Company that was owned by York Enterprises.

CHAPTER 47

Blackness washed all around as Lisa struggled to sit up. A throbbing bruise pulsated against her cheek as she rolled over on the cold wooden floor. Each move of her limbs was like pushing through a sea of molasses, her hands and legs falling behind each shift of her body. Her face was pressed against the floor and a heavy smell of disinfectant mixed with a thick scent of rust permeated the wooden planks and the combination made her feel ill.

A dullness filled each sound out of her throat and also brought with it a raw pounding in her skull. She eventually pushed herself up from the floor, feeling in the dark for support, and toppling a table sideways.

Lisa lurched forward, her stomach released its contents, and the painful dizziness dulled to a swirl. She grabbed hold of her stomach, wiped the sickness from her chin, and screamed for help.

A sliver of light stretched across the floor, slowly illuminating the room as a door opened.

“You’re finally awake,” the man’s voice was calm, and he seemed unsurprised by Lisa’s cries for help.

“Who are you?” The words slurred from her mouth and her lids fought to remain open, threatening to pull her back into another unconscious slumber. “What do you want with me?”

Each step he took echoed in the room, and Lisa focused on the boots that approached from the far end of the room as her eyes adjusted to the light.

He stopped next to the overturned table and crouched down, tilting Lisa's face up to meet his.

"It looks like you aren't feeling well," he said as he wiped the base of her chin.

He slid his hands under her arms and lifted her off the floor. With surprising gentleness, her abductor carried her to the sofa and lowered her body onto the cushions.

"What do you want with me?" Lisa asked, pulling back her arms when he reached out to touch her.

The sound of a deep, baritone horn blew in the distance and Lisa struggled to remember where she recognized it from. She looked around the room but nothing looked familiar.

"The less you know the better," the man lowered himself into a chair across from where Lisa was stretched out on the sofa.

"I don't understand," Lisa rubbed the side of her head, the pounding in her skull overtaking the violent twisting in her stomach. "Why me?" Her voice wobbled.

"I need your help."

"Why would I help you?" Lisa snapped.

"Because you want to live."

His answer was calm and direct and Lisa knew it came from a man who was willing to end her life if he didn't get what he wanted.

"I don't even know how I can help you, I own a small coffee shop in town, I'm not exactly in a position to help anyone."

"I was listening to you the other day as you spoke with your friend," he leaned forward, resting his arms on his knees. "The one who's helping the police with the investigations."

"Kerry?" Lisa's vision cleared and she recognized the man who was in her café the day she was abducted. "You said you were just passing through on your way to the east coast. I'm going to guess that was a lie."

The man smiled and Lisa recoiled at the sight of his grin. A sense of evil emanated from him, something her grandmother would always refer to as a 'weird feeling' she'd get when she was around people she thought would do her harm. This man, sitting across from her was giving her that same warning sense of evil.

"I want you to dial her number," he tossed a phone onto the sofa cushion.

"And if I don't?"

"You don't want to know."

"What do you want with her?" Lisa wondered if this was the man who tried to grab Dominique.

"I want you to tell them to call off the investigation."

"They won't do that," Lisa said.

The evil grin returned, "I just need them to think that's what I want. The point is to distract them enough so what I came here to do is finished. Now call."

The phone was heavy in Lisa's hand and her vision was weak from the drug he had used to knock her out.

Lisa dialed her friend's number and listened to each ring until a horn in the distance blew and she finally heard Kerry's voice.

CHAPTER 48

Kerry walked out of the room, covering her right ear to block out the sound of the printer, and shouted into the phone, “Lisa, is that you?”

“Kerry, I ...” only two words escaped Lisa’s mouth before the phone was yanked away from her hand.

“Is this Doctor Dearborne?” the voice was low and hollow and eerily calm following the worry in Lisa’s voice.

“Who is this?” Kerry yelled.

“The person who’s holding your friend’s life in his hands.”

"What do you want?"

"I want you to convince the police to back off of their investigation into the two murders."

"I can't do that," Kerry said. "They're close to figuring out who you are."

"We both know that's not the truth."

"Who are you? Why did you even kill those two men?"

"I think you referred to me as the sick twisted weakling," he said, followed by a low laugh, "That should tell you all you need to know."

"Why don't you let Lisa go? She has nothing to do with the investigation. Hurting her will only make things worse for you once the police catch you."

"I'll release her once there's a statement made by the police saying that they are pausing their investigation and that they've hit a dead-end in their search for the killer."

"They won't do that."

"Then convince them, because your friend's life is in their hands. You have until the end of the day."

The call abruptly ended, but not before Kerry heard Lisa's cry and a low deep horn blow in the distance.

Kerry opened up her phone's call history and the number that had just called her registered as unknown. When she pressed *69 to initiate a callback, there was no answer. She pressed Simon's contact number, noticing the time and realizing he was at the property at East River Bridge. Her panicked voice and hurried speech cut into Simon's words.

"Calm down, Kerry," Simon said. "Slow down and tell me what happened. You said Lisa called?"

"Yes, but I only heard her voice for a few seconds then the man who took her came on the line," Kerry cried. "He said he'd hurt her if you didn't call off your investigation."

Simon climbed into his car and Kerry could hear the door slam shut as the ignition started.

"I'm on my way back, Peter can handle the search of the property and field. Meet me at the station."

Kerry rushed out the door and raced over to the station, arriving a short while before Simon and Josh.

"Give me your phone, I'll have Jamie see if he can trace the number," Simon took Kerry's phone and handed it off to Jamie who plugged it into his computer.

"Tell us exactly what was said. Go slowly and don't leave anything out."

Simon, Josh, and Sally were poised around the desk.

"I was printing some results from the soil testing when my phone rang. The number came up as unknown but that's not unusual since I get a lot of calls to my phone," Kerry explained. "Lisa only got a few words out before the guy who kidnapped her came on the line. He said that if you didn't make a formal statement that you were ending the search for who killed Paul and David that he'd hurt Lisa. And I really think he'll do it."

"Okay, back up," Simon said. "Tell me about his voice."

"His voice?" Kerry shook her head. "Um, he was calm, in a scary way. Like he knew that you were nowhere close to finding him. He was young, too. Maybe in his twenties, but it was hard to tell."

"What else?" Simon prompted Kerry's memory. "Were there any other sounds you could identify?"

Kerry sat forward, "There was a horn. I don't know what kind, but it was deep. Like a foghorn."

Simon looked at Josh, "Do you know where there's a foghorn in Lake Pines?"

Josh shook his head, "Even if there was one, there wouldn't be any use for it today."

Jamie returned with Kerry's phone and handed it to Simon, "I got the number for the phone that called Kerry, it's a prepaid mobile phone. I can trace where it was purchased and how he paid for it, but it will take a while."

"Okay, get started on that and let me know as soon as you find anything out," Simon said.

"Sounds good," Jamie turned around, and just before he reached the hall Simon called out.

"Hey, do you know anywhere in Lake Pines that has a foghorn?"

"The only place I can think of that has a foghorn is The Old Barge."

"What old barge?"

"No, *The Old Barge*," Jamie corrected Simon. "It's the name of a floating bar. The guy who owns it makes his way around the lake, he's never in one place for too long."

"I've never heard of it."

"Yeah, it's kind of an alternative bar," Jamie explained.

"You mean it's an illegal bar."

Jamie nodded.

"How do we find out where The Old Barge is now?" Simon asked. "Kerry heard a foghorn when she was on the phone with the guy who is holding Lisa."

"There's an underground network. Let me put some feelers out and I'll figure out where it is," Jamie raced back to his computer.

"Until then, we can rule him out as the serial killer from the 70s because of his age," Simon said.

"And we can rule out Nick Hindley as being responsible for killing Paul Morrow and David Woodward," Josh said.

"Oliver and Thomas positively identified him in the line-up last night. Vicky Chan is coming in this morning to see if she recognizes him," Josh said.

"Actually, she's here now," Sally said. "Jayson was placing Nick in a lineup just before you arrived."

Simon rushed to the back room and ran into Jayson as he was leading Vicky out of the viewing room and down the hall.

"Vicky, thanks for coming in," Simon stretched out his arm and shook her hand. "Did you recognize anyone?"

Vicky shook her head, "No, I'm sorry."

"That's alright, thanks for giving it a shot," he said. "Sorry for making you come out on such a chilly evening."

"I really thought I would see that Dan kid in the lineup," Vicky said.

"Dan?"

"Yeah, some kid I hired to do some odd jobs around the studio," Vicky explained. "He applied for a job as a general assistant a few months ago. I needed someone to help me organize the studio. I've been so busy that it was hard to keep up with cleaning, and keeping track of my storage room. I was misplacing invoices and I could only take on more jobs if I had some help."

"What happened to him?" Simon asked. "He obviously doesn't work for you anymore if you were prepared to see him today."

"I had to let him go," Vicky said. "He had a really good portfolio of landscape photos and I was planning on having him work with some clients in the summer. You know, taking family portraits or professional headshots for businesses but I wanted to make sure he had the right attitude and that he'd be a good fit with my clients. He said he was getting frustrated doing grunt work around the studio. I ended up firing him when I realized supplies were going missing from my studio. Plus, after a while, I just never felt comfortable around him when we were alone."

"Do you have a last name or some contact information?"

"I hate to admit it, but I agreed to pay him cash," Vicky explained. "He seemed to prefer being paid that way and it saved me some money in taxes. But, I think I still have his phone number."

Vicky pulled her phone out of her purse and found the number that was listed under his first name.

Simon recognized the number as the same prepaid mobile cell phone that Jamie had traced to Kerry's phone.

"Do you think you could describe him to our sketch artist?"

"Yeah, of course," Vicky smiled. "I never forget a face."

"One more thing," Simon said as he walked Vicky over to the sketch artist's desk. "You said that you suspected Dan of stealing some items from your studio. What did he steal."

"Weird things," Vicky recalled. "He took some photo studio props, a box of pencils, and some jugs of disinfectant."

CHAPTER 49

Lake Pines was becoming cocooned in the spring storm that had pushed into the region, getting rapidly worse by the minute and threatening the search for Lisa. The sketch artist had completed her drawing based on Vicky's description of Dan and it would be sent out to every officer and scanned through the police database.

"If Dan was arrested, then his information will show up in the system," Simon explained. "I'm running a Canada-wide search and Vicky is looking through her files back at her studio to see if she can find anything else. Like his last name or an address."

Kerry looked at the time, something they all had been vigilantly watching.

"What are we going to do if we don't find out where he's holding Lisa?" Kerry nervously paced around the desk. "I feel silly just waiting around."

Simon put his hands on Kerry's shoulders and she stopped moving, "We all do. The important thing is to keep a clear head so we'll be ready when we get some information."

Josh looked out the window, "That storm has finally hit the area."

Everyone turned around, surprised to see the flurry of snow drifting by the window. With everyone's focus on figuring out who took Lisa and where she was being held, no one had realized that a massive storm was moving through the area and had coated the town with a layer of heavy snow. Thick, wet snow pounded against the window, and taps from icy grains rhythmically beat against the glass. Clumps of ice clung to the edge of the window frame while smaller flakes of snow melted upon hitting the warmed glass and slid down to the ledge.

Any daylight that would have helped officers in their search was quickly disappearing behind the heavy cloud cover.

The call came into Simon's phone as he was wiping fog off the window, "Vicky, I'm hoping your call means that you found something."

Simon grabbed a pen and wrote down the address that Vicky found in her journal dating back to the first week she had hired Dan. He thanked Vicky and then after he called for additional back-up he and Josh rushed out the doors and drove directly to Dan's home, hoping that they weren't too late to save Lisa.

CHAPTER 50

Police cars surrounded the yellow bungalow at the end of the cul-de-sac next to the old stone church. Folsum Cove was built on a ridge at the highest point in town and in one of the original neighborhoods in Lake Pines. Nestled close to a park that overlooked the lake from its position on the top of a hill, the neighborhood that locals had referred to as Silver Heights was a popular location for the more senior residents in their town.

Rotating red and blue lights reflected off the backdrop of the heavy snow that obscured the seven homes that curved around the road. A crescent of bungalows with skinny front driveways built for a generation that would never own more than one car, faced into a small circle of grass in the middle of the street. It was too small to be called a park but just large enough to support a large oak tree that was planted in the center of it.

Drapes were partially pulled back from the front windows of neighboring homes, onlookers shielding themselves from the implication that something illegal was happening on their street.

Tensions were already high in the small community, with citizens feeling vulnerable in their own homes. Learning of the recent murders gave everyone reason to pause and reassess their own security, however, it was the discovery of thirty-one bodies in a popular and much loved public park that caused the most upset. There was a recent upswell in believing that their obliviousness of what had happened in their close-knit town made them complicit in the crime. And everyone's guilt was shrouded in fear, not because of the two recent murders but of the truth that was sure to surface from the older crime.

The house at number eleven Folsum Cove was dark. It was one of the few homes without a light illuminating the front porch. Approaching rapidly but silently, the officers surrounded the home. Once everyone was in position, Simon knocked on the door and called out, announcing their presence. When there was no response after the second knock, Simon gave the signal and officers burst through the front and back doors of the home.

The woman's cry was followed by shattering glass as three officers stormed into the main floor of the small house. Screaming and pulling her long fluffy peach-colored robe over her legs, an elderly woman backed up against the fridge in the corner of her kitchen.

Simon lowered his weapon, told the officers to stand down, and then guided the woman to a chair.

"What's going on?" the woman looked down at the shattered glass on the kitchen floor.

Simon lowered himself into a chair next to the woman while the officers searched the home.

"Does someone by the name of Dan live here?" Simon asked. "We knocked twice and called out, but there was no response."

"Dan? Is that why you're here?" the woman cradled her torso with her shaking arms.

"Yes, does he live here?"

The woman nodded, "But I don't understand? He's never been a problem, in fact, he's the quietest border I've ever had."

"Border? He's not your son or grandson?"

"Oh, heavens, no. I rent out my basement to help make ends meet. Dan has been quiet as a church mouse," the old woman explained. "You must have the wrong place."

"When was the last time you saw him?" Simon asked.

The woman looked past Simon and watched as an officer headed down the hall, "Where are they going?"

"We need to find Dan," Simon said. "Do you know where he is?"

The woman shook her head, "He left two days ago. He said he was going back home to visit his aunt who had taken ill and he said he didn't know when he'd be back."

"Which room is his?"

"He rented the basement," the woman said. "It has a kitchen, laundry, and a separate entrance."

Simon instructed an officer to stay with the woman he now knew as Gertrude and took two officers and headed down the stairs.

"You've made a mistake," Gertrude yelled out. "Dan's a kind young man. He wouldn't hurt a fly."

Simon pushed open the door at the bottom of the landing and turned on the light as he and three officers stepped into Dan's private apartment. Their eyes went directly to the wall of photos that were pinned into the grooved paneling.

Spanning an entire length of the room, the images confirmed that they had arrived at the right house. And Gertrude's impression of who the young man she rented her basement to was a far cry from the kind soul she protested he was. They had arrived at the lair of a monster.

CHAPTER 51

A nauseous realization washed over every officer in the room that the man who had kidnapped Lisa was also the same person who murdered Paul Morrow and David Woodward. Categorized in an organized flow chart, pictures of five men were pinned to the wall.

At the top was a picture of Paul Morrow. His placement in the chart confirmed that he was the initial victim. The attack and the facets of the crime were plotted out in extreme detail and typed neatly on a page next to his image.

"These must have been some of the photos from Vicky's studio?" Simon said as he and Josh took in the horrors displayed on the wall. "And he wasn't going to finish by only killing Paul and David."

Below Paul's image, and at the bottom of a thin black line was a picture of David Woodward. Artistically posing in the same exercise gear that had become his trademark work apparel, David was balancing on a rock at the water's edge.

Three more images followed David's, along with a sheet filled with their personal information. Each target and victim were organized in the same manner.

There was also the outline for how he would lure each of the men to a secluded area. Paul was offered a side job building a dock, which explained his absence from work and home. David was hired on the false pretense to run a private session for a wealthy cottage owner who wanted to remain anonymous. Both men he had initially met while working at Vicky Chan's studio.

"Let's contact these other three men and make sure they're safe," Simon pointed to the wall. "And If they are, station a police officer at each of their homes for extra security."

Josh stared at the wall, "Let's hope that they're still alive."

"Lisa's not on this wall," Simon noticed. "They're all Vicky's clients. Look at the bottom right-hand corner of the pictures, it has her studio logo printed on them."

"That's how Dan met each of his victims. While he was working at Vicky's studio," Josh said.

"Then why Lisa?" Simon asked.

Simon moved along the wall, reading each typed sheet and examining each photograph on the wall. He stopped when he reached the portion of the wall that displayed newspaper clippings. They included the recent reports of the discovery of Paul and David's bodies along with photocopied images of older articles. But it was the picture of the familiar building and the note taped to the bottom of it that worried Simon the most.

CHAPTER 52

Simon's phone vibrated in his pocket, and without taking his eyes off the image and the note on the wall, he answered the call.

"We got a hit on the sketch we uploaded to the police database," Sally said. "His name is Dan Harold. He was arrested for a DUI last year. We also have his address of where he's been living in Lake Pines, it's the same one that Vicky gave you."

"Yeah, I know Sally," Simon's voice was filled with dread once he realized the reason Dan Harold was in Lake Pines.

"We found proof that he's the one who killed Paul and David."

"Well, there's something else you need to know. There was also a long note and a file attached by Dan's parole officer," Sally said. "Since it was Dan's first offense and he was a young student, the judge went easy on him and gave him community service. He was teaching photography at the corrections facility."

"Let me guess, he was placed at the same facility where Kaylum Randall is being held."

"That's right. How did you know?" Sally asked.

"Because I'm looking at a collection of photos of the facility and one recent portrait that was done of Kaylum Randall," Simon said. "There's also a letter that Kaylum wrote to Dan. In it, he told him that he's like the son he never had and he flourishes Dan with praise for his work at the facility."

"Do you have any idea of where he's keeping Lisa?" Sally asked. "We're all just sitting on pins and needles over here."

Simon focused on a picture of a small cabin that was affixed to the wall. He recognized the same large rock that David was posing on and the same crooked tree that Paul was leaning against in his picture.

If his hunch was right he was looking at the location where Paul and David were murdered and where Lisa was now being held.

CHAPTER 53

A forensic team was collecting the images and evidence from Gertrude's basement where Dan Harold had been living and planning his murders. After she packed a small bag, an officer walked a shocked and frightened Gertrude to her neighbor's house where she broke down in tears as she explained why she needed a place to sleep for the night.

Simon and Josh returned to the station, hoping to narrow down the location of the cabin where they were certain Lisa was being held.

Jamie rushed into the room, waving his phone just as Simon tossed his snow-covered coat on the back of a chair.

"I have the owner of The Old Barge on the line," Jamie handed his phone to Simon. "I told him you weren't interested in what he was doing, just that you wanted some info. I hope that's alright?"

Simon nodded and grabbed the phone from Jamie, "Hi, who am I speaking with?"

"Jamie said I wouldn't have to give you my name," the man on the other end of the line sounded like he was the same age as Jamie and he spoke with a slow drawl.

"We think that you may have been in the area where a woman is being held," Simon explained. "We need to find her and we wanted to narrow down our search."

"Yeah, Jamie told me," the man said. "Fire away, what do you want to know?"

Simon put the phone on speaker, "For starters, can you blow your foghorn. I want to see if it's the same one that one of our witnesses heard over the phone."

The owner of The Old Barge did as Simon asked and a loud, deep horn echoed through the speakers of Jamie's phone, and Kerry nodded her head, "That was the same horn."

"What part of the lake were you on today?" Simon asked and then recalled the slow speech and wondered how much the driver of The Old Barge would remember. "It's really important that you're accurate."

"I can do one better. I'll send you the route I took. I wasn't too far out since I was only sticking to areas where the ice had completely melted on the lake. I record it on my account so customers can find out where I'm going to be." Following his admission, he cursed his stupidity. "You're not going to use that against me, are you?"

"Just send me the info."

Within a few seconds an image of a small section of the lake, and an outlet of a creek showed a green dotted line that marked out the destination The Old Barge took from seven o'clock in the morning, right up to when Simon was speaking with him on the phone.

The line was marked with red locator dots stamped with the time, marking the barge's movement at half-hour intervals.

"Did you get the map?"

"Yeah, the point in time that we got the call, your barge was in Laurensons Lake," Simon grabbed the photo he took from Dan's apartment. "I'm going to send you a picture of a cabin, can you let me know if you recognize it?"

Simon sent the photo and immediately the man who ran the illegal party barge confirmed that the cabin was built on the sharp curve that turned north on Laurensons Lake.

CHAPTER 54

As Simon drove, Josh was on the phone with the supervisor at the corrections facility where Kaylum Randall was being held since 1974 and where Dan Harold was teaching photography to inmates as a fulfillment of his community service.

"How long has Dan been volunteering with the inmates?" Josh asked, the call on speaker as everyone listened in.

"Just under a year," the administrator said. "He finished his service about two weeks ago."

"Did you ever have any problems with him?" Josh asked.

"Like what?"

"Did he cause any problems for you or any of the inmates?"

"No, actually he was able to get some of the more reclusive guys involved."

"Did he work with Kaylum Randall?"

"Oh, yeah," the supervisor said. "He was such a miserable guy to be around, always chirping about his meals being cold or being treated poorly. You'd think these guys were away at a spa retreat. Anyway, Dan was able to get Kaylum Randall interested in photography and it seemed to take the edge off of him."

Once Josh was certain that there was nothing new the supervisor could add to Dan's profile, Josh thanked him and ended the call.

"Kaylum Randall is due in front of the judge in an hour," Simon said. "If we don't find Dan and get Peter to have that hearing stopped, we could have two killers out on the street."

"That's why Dan was in such a rush to have you announce that you were ending your investigation by the end of the day," Kerry said. "I bet he was trying to draw attention away from Kaylum's hearing."

"It's not the first time that a stranger has become infatuated with a prisoner and has been willing to do anything to get them freed."

"Even commit two murders that mirror the ones that Kaylum Randall was accused, tried, and sentenced for committing?"

“Especially that,” Simon said. “By Dan copying the signature murders of the serial killer cases in the 70s, it put a shadow of doubt on the charges against Kaylum. Once we found a connection between the two murders, then it was only a matter of time before Kaylum’s lawyer was going to push for his sentence to be overturned.”

“It explains how Dan learned the intimate details of the killings. Kaylum probably even told Dan about the bodies in Belvedere Field.”

Simon pushed his foot down on the accelerator and increase the speed of the wipers. Snow was clinging to the rubber blades, marking blurry streaks across the windshield. In the distance, they could see three cabins, all with soft lights illuminating the inside.

"Vicky said that Dan drove a small black hatchback," Simon said. "She wasn't sure of the make."

"There," Kerry shoved her arm between Josh and Simon as she leaned forward from the backseat of the car. "The smallest cabin on the left."

They approached without sirens or flashing lights. Three cars followed behind Simon and he directed them over the radio to move to opposite sides so they could quietly surround the cabin.

The wind had subsided and the major storm that was initially anticipated turned into what meteorologists were dubbing a bomb cyclone. Across North America, the harsh winter morphed into a spring filled with raging storms that lasted only a few hours but left a trail of destruction in its wake. Record amounts of snowfall and hurricane-strength winds cut power to major cities and caused the cancelation of numerous flights. So far, all that Lake Pines had to contend with was extra shoveling.

Simon parked under the dense cover of a row of pine trees and pulled out his phone.

"I'll dial the number once everyone is in position, and then wait for my signal," Simon spoke into the radio and each officer acknowledge Simon's plan.

Simon turned his body around and leaned over the back seat toward Kerry, "Stay here."

Kerry had no intention of following Simon and the others. She reached out and grabbed his arm, "Be careful."

Kerry watched as the officers moved closer to the cabin, dressed in black and the silhouettes of their brandished guns held in front of their bodies. Simon raised his arm, signaling for each of the officers to hold their position, and then dialed the number.

The call was answered, and deep breathing was all Simon could hear at the end of the line. He waited for Dan to make a sound, but instead, he heard Lisa's cry as Dan pushed her toward the phone and shouted for her to speak.

"Hello?"

Simon instantly recognized Lisa's voice, having known her for so many years. It was a frail, frightened version of the woman he only knew as jovial and carefree. As painful as it was to hear the terror in her voice, it meant that she was still alive.

"Lisa, are you okay?" Simon asked.

"Simon!" Lisa shouted into the phone which was quickly yanked from her hands.

"Where's Kerry?" Dan snapped.

Simon could see a face peer out from the cabin as he pulled the corner of the drape back.

"We have you surrounded," Simon said. "Let Lisa go and we'll talk about how we can bring you in without any gunfire."

The drape was pulled shut, "I was very clear when I spoke with Kerry. I want you to call off the investigation and I want you to make the announcement public."

"That's not going to happen, Dan," Simon said. "Now release Lisa and we can talk."

"How do you know my name?" the confidence and cockiness that Dan spoke with earlier had disappeared and desperation filled his voice.

"I know a lot about you Dan," Simon stepped around a clump of trees and moved closer to the cabin, and crouched below the car. Simon waved his arm, signaling the two officers nearest the front of the cabin to approach the porch. Simon continued to speak, hoping to distract Dan from the officers' movements. "We already know you're responsible for the murders of Paul Morrow and David Woodward but now we know why you did it. It was to help free Kaylum Randall."

"You don't know what you're talking about!" Dan shouted.

"Kaylum told us that he convinced you to commit the murders so he could use the crimes to try and get released. He said you were such an easy target because you were so enamored with him."

"He didn't convince me to do anything," Dan shouted. "Anything I did, I did on my own."

Simon recognized the sound of bravado and ego in Dan's tone and decided to capitalize on it.

"That's not what he said earlier today when we spoke with him."

The line fell silent and Simon motioned for the officers to step closer and then hold their position. He wanted to make sure that Lisa wouldn't be injured in a rushed attempt to capture Dan.

Simon continued, “We confronted Kaylum with what we knew and he said you weren’t smart enough to see through what he was trying to do. He said he picked you because he believed you wouldn’t be bright enough to think for yourself and once he was out, he was going to turn you in.”

“I’m the one who gave him the idea. I’m the one who promised to take care of everything that would make sure he’d be freed,” Dan’s screams morphed into sobs. “I even buried the first body in his favorite field!”

“That’s not what Kaylum said,” Simon continued his lie as he stepped closer to the cabin, hoping he would weaken Dan's resolve. “He said you were an embarrassment and that he regretted ever telling you anything. Plus, your plan didn't work because an hour ago the judge ruled against him and sent him back to jail."

"He was lazy, that's why he was caught," Dan yelled. "He said that if he kept pushing his innocence and continued to file for release that eventually the court would see that he was framed by the cop who arrested him. But it was my idea to commit copycat murders which would raise doubt with the court. If it was left up to him, he'd die in that prison."

"And what did you expect would happen once he was out?" Simon asked. "You may have thought that Kaylum was going to take you under his wing, but he had already planned to turn you in."

A loud crash came from inside, and then Dan screamed, "Hey, what are you doing? Let go!"

Lisa jumped on Dan when he was distracted on the phone, giving Simon the opportunity he was waiting for. Simon waved his arm and every officer ran into the cabin. Simon, Josh, and two others from the front, and two from the back.

Kerry watched as the front door flew open. She jumped out of the car and ran toward the cabin and the echo of shouts carried through the cold stillness of the early evening. Everything fell silent after the sound of gunshots and Kerry ran toward the cabin, slipping along the icy path and catapulting herself onto the porch. Josh rushed out the door and held Kerry back just as another shot was fired.

Kerry stood, motionless, as Josh kept her from entering the cabin, and just as she was about to push free, Simon walked around the door holding his arm around Lisa's shoulders.

Kerry threw her arms around Simon and Lisa, believing only a second earlier one of them had been shot.

"It's all over," Simon pulled Lisa out of the cabin and Josh guided her to the police car while he radioed the station.

"Who was shot?" Kerry asked.

"Dan," Simon leaned into the cabin and gave the four officers instructions on securing the crime scene. "Dan got off a shot when the first officer burst through the door, but thankfully it missed him. One of the officers who ran in through the back shot him when he saw Dan pointing a gun at Lisa. He saved her life."

Kerry pulled her coat closed and let out a breath that escaped in a frozen cloud surrounding her face.

A few feet from the front door of the cabin, Dan Harold lay on the floor, framed in a pool of blood.

They searched the cabin and found the room where Dan had murdered Paul Morrow and David Woodward. The small room was covered in plastic, and the bathtub was filled with the disinfectant that he submerged the bodies of his victims with after they were killed. Simon was certain that once the forensic team gathered samples, the blood splatters would match those of Paul Morrow and David Woodward.

On the counter, in a neat pile were the missing belongings of the two men he killed and a small package of chrysanthemum seeds. Confirming without a doubt that this was where they died and that Dan Harold was the one who killed them.

As Simon walked through the living room he glanced at the pictures that lined the mantle. They belonged to the owner of the cabin, who Simon realized was the same woman who rented Dan the basement suite in her home.

"This cabin belongs to his landlady," Simon said. "I have a feeling she's not going to want to take in any more borders once she learns everything that Dan Harold did."

Simon left the cabin and walked Kerry down the icy path.

"You go with Lisa," Simon said. "I have to call Peter and then secure the cabin. I'll be here for a few more hours."

Kerry walked back to the police car and climbed in the back seat beside Lisa. She wrapped her arm around her friend and as Josh started the car and pulled away from the cabin, she looked back and watched as Simon walked back into the cabin. The murder investigation of Paul Morrow and David Woodward was solved but the horror of what Dan Harold had done would remain behind forever.

CHAPTER 55

Kaylum Randall made it three feet from the judge. His lawyer was successful in obtaining the last time slot in the day for the preliminary argument that they both hoped would lead to Kaylum's conviction being overturned.

With a smug smile on his face, believing that Dan Harold had succeeded in his plan, Kaylum stared at the judge as he professed his innocence. He told lies of his terror-filled nights laying on a cold cot wondering if he'd be killed while he slept. Fellow prisoners, who threatened him regularly, had followed through with beatings so severe that they warranted several visits to the infirmary and had left him with numbness in his arm and a permanent limp in his left leg.

Kaylum's story of woe and innocence was interrupted by a court clerk who approached the provincial prosecutor with a note which she in turn handed to the judge.

Everyone in the courtroom was certain the judge was holding back his smile as he read out the contents of the note.

Dan Harold had been killed earlier that afternoon while he held an innocent woman hostage. Not only did he confess to the murders of Paul Morrow and David Woodward, but he admitted the plan contrived between him and Kaylum

Randall after the two spent time together during a volunteer photography class in prison.

Proof of their plan was found on Dan's phone when he had recorded Kaylum and him talking during a photography class. Proof Dan wanted to have in case Kaylum Randall ever tried to betray him.

In addition to being returned to prison, charges were being brought against Kaylum Randall based on the proof that was also found in the storage boxes at his house. As it turned out, the judge informed a despondent and angered Kaylum Randall, he was being charged for the desecration of the graves of thirty-one remains.

Kaylum flew into a rage when the additional charges were read out by the judge and he was quickly taken away. His hands were cuffed and he screamed wildly as his lawyer informed the court that he was resigning as Kaylum Randall's lawyer. Citing that his client persisted in instructing him to act contrary to his sworn professional ethics.

Kaylum silenced his fitful rage and then leaned close to the lawyer and said, "You'll pay for this."

The lawyer's jaw tensed and the cold, steely eyes of a killer stared back at him and he knew he had made a mistake to take the case to defend Kaylum Randall in 1974.

It was the lawyer's DUI conviction that the arresting officer was holding over his head when he visited him in his office and told him to take the case. There was a clear understanding that Kaylum Randall was to be found guilty. Even though the true killer was put behind bars, it always perplexed the lawyer why the arresting officer risked breaking the law to ensure it would happen. The officer's name had been seared into his memory, and now that he was the Commissioner of the Provincial Police, there was no way to forget it.

CHAPTER 56

Peter put down the phone and his shoulders dropped as a grin stretched across his face, "That was Commissioner Robertson. We got the message to the judge in time. In addition to Kaylum Randall being returned to prison, there were additional charges brought against him for moving the bodies from the property at East River Bridge."

"And Josh confirmed that the other men who were also targeted by Dan Harold are all safe," Simon dropped down into a chair and stretched his arms above his head. "Kerry went with Lisa to the hospital while she's being examined. Thankfully, it looked like she received only minor scrapes and bruises when she was kidnapped. It'll be the deeper scars of the trauma of what happened that will be with her for some time to come."

"I'll talk to her," Josh said. "I've been seeing a therapist, which has helped me a lot."

Simon sat forward, "What? Why?"

"It's been more difficult to deal with Wayne's death than I've been letting on," Josh explained. "I was trying to stay strong for Lucia and I didn't want to let anyone down. Not only had I started a new job when I moved back to Lake Pines, but I was also stepping into my brother's shoes, and that was a huge challenge."

"I didn't know," Simon said. "You don't have to deal with this alone, Kerry and I will always be there for you."

Peter placed his hand on Josh's shoulder, "That includes me, too."

"Thanks," Josh said. "The first step was to let Thomas know, once I did, it was a lot easier to open up. Being busy has also helped, I'm just glad we were able to stop Kaylum Randall from having his case overturned."

"Thankfully that didn't happen," Simon looked past Josh, and into the hall.

"What is it?" Josh asked, recognizing the look on Simon's face.

"Nick Hindley."

"What about him?"

"There's nothing to connect him to either Dan Howard or to Kaylum Randall, and when you sat down with him yesterday, he still refused to reveal what information he had to offer," Simon said. "He made it seem that whatever information he had it would help him avoid harsh charges for attacking Kerry and trying to kidnap Dominique."

Josh stood, "We're on a roll tonight, and I don't think that anyone is going to sleep soon. Let's give it another shot."

Peter agreed, "I'll sit in with Josh, maybe my presence will make him believe that he has a chance at making a deal."

With Simon shielded by the viewing glass, Josh and Peter waited in the interrogation room while a guard walked Nick Hindley down from his cell.

The door to the small room opened, and Nick sauntered inside and sat down at the table. He looked at Josh and then at Peter and groaned as the guard tugged his arm as he tightened one end of his handcuffs to the table. His face was smeared with a white ointment and the edges of the burn were beginning to heal.

Josh introduced Peter and Nick's eyes widened at the presence of the Superintendent.

"Why am I here?" Nick asked.

"The last time we spoke you implied that you had information that we may be interested in," Josh said.

"I didn't imply, I straight out told you I had info that you would want," Nick snapped. "But it'll cost you."

"You still haven't retained a lawyer," Josh flipped through Nick's arrest file.

"I don't need one."

"I disagree," Josh said. "Kidnapping and assault are very serious charges. Especially with your track record of arrests."

Josh waited while Nick considered his options, which were few. Josh couldn't help but recognize the tough exterior and bravado that Nick Hindley displayed the first time he interrogated him was crumbling. Before him now sat a frightened man, well aware of the future jail time he was facing because of the attack on Kerry, and Dominique's attempted kidnapping. His eyes darted around the room and his teeth gnawed at a raw scab, now bleeding, as he bit down on his lower lip.

"Okay, fine, get me one of your free lawyers and I'll tell you what I know."

“Before we even consider talking about a deal, we’re going to need proof that what you have to tell us is of value.”

Nick leaned forward and rested his loose arm as comfortably as he could on the surface of the table, “It has to do with the man who killed Officer Burgess. I know where he is.”

CHAPTER 57

Josh held his breath and pushed his fist down on his lap as the guard unlocked Nick's arm from the leg of the table. He waited until Nick was out of the room and out of view before he let out a gasp and looked at Peter. Simon ran in from the next room.

"What's he talking about? Alex Johnson has been in prison since we arrested him on the dock in Thunder Bay."

"Are you sure?" Josh asked. "Nick seemed pretty confident that he had the right information, and he knew we would want it."

Peter was already making the call and within minutes he had confirmed their nightmare.

"Alex Johnson escaped two weeks ago," Peter said. "He was being transferred to the hospital after he came down with a fever. He overpowered the guard who was with him and it was a couple of hours before they realized he was gone."

"Why didn't we hear about this? Why weren't we alerted?" Josh asked.

"He had been transferred to a prison in British Columbia shortly after his arrest, and the search has been contained to that province," Peter said. "There was no reason for him to return to Lake Pines. The RCMP thought this would be the last place he'd come if he wanted to remain hidden."

"Then why does Nick Hindley claim to know where he is?" Simon asked.

"Or more importantly," Josh added. "Why is Nick here in Lake Pines?"

CHAPTER 58

For the third time that morning, Kerry forced herself to refocus on the files in front of her. Thirty-one bodies were found in Belvedere Field. All of them were relocated from their original graves and then reburied by Kaylum Randall. One was the doctor coordinating the medical tests in the secretive facility, the thirty that remained were all children. The first to be positively identified was Adam Thibert.

Twenty-nine victims, buried in unmarked graves, were waiting to be identified. Silently pleading from the room they were stored in. Except for the shroud of canvas that their small bodies were buried in, none were left with connections to who they were or the lives they lived.

But no matter how nagging the pull was for Kerry to focus on the remains and to match them to possible missing children reports, she couldn't forget what Simon had told her when he returned home.

Nick Hindley, the man who attacked her and tried to abduct their daughter, had information on the man who had murdered Wayne.

Perplexed and angered, Simon spent a fitful night tossing and turning in bed, while Kerry lay awake with the knowledge of why she and Dominique were a target.

She had concealed the information of who Alex Johnson was, believing that he'd remain in prison, and never learn about Dominique's existence or his connection to the young girl. Kerry had pulled the document out of the locked safe in her office and stared at it for a half-hour, trying to figure out how she would explain everything to Simon.

When she received the information on Dominique's birth father, Kerry was terrified to learn that he was instrumental in a large human trafficking ring as well as the man responsible for killing Wayne.

What began as an altruistic search to learn more about Dominique's birth family had turned into a harrowing nightmare. One she thought had been put behind them when Alex was arrested, and eventually convicted.

Returning the envelope to the safe didn't remove its presence in her mind, but Kerry focused on the pressing issue at hand. The twenty-nine remains that required identification.

Dental records were able to confirm the identity of Doctor Alpin and six children. The bracelet led Kerry to Adam Thibert's file, and a final DNA match with his mother confirmed his identity.

Kerry knew that many of the missing children reports that were not solved were of children found missing from rural communities. They were from areas where families may not have had access to regular dental exams. Facial recognition was going to be her first step toward matching a set of remains to a child, then, and only then, would she contact the family to collect samples of their DNA. The last thing she wanted to do was to inflict further pain and suffering on the families by giving them false hope or forcing them to remember the loss of their child.

The process was slow and tedious but extremely distracting, which Kerry was initially grateful for after Nick Hindley's latest revelation. But the time came when she could no longer avoid telling Simon the information she had on Dominique's birth father.

When she dialed Simon's number, Kerry held her breath. It wasn't until Simon confirmed that Nick Hindley had been hired by Alex Johnson to kidnap

Dominique that Kerry knew she had to come clean.

"I know why Alex targeted Dominique, and it's not because of you arresting him," Kerry let out a deep breath.

Kerry explained that when she set out to learn more about Dominique's birth mother, she had no idea a monster would turn out to be connected to their daughter. Kerry didn't learn Alex was Dominique's birth father until after his arrest for his role in the human trafficking ring. Believing that Alex would remain behind bars for the rest of his life, Kerry decided to keep Alex's connection to Dominique hidden. Simon was Dominique's father, and the idea of a monster like Alex having anything to do with their daughter terrified her. Simon agreed that to reveal their knowledge of why Nick Handley was in Lake Pines would be to place Dominique in danger.

Simon didn't speak for what seemed like a long time and then in a calm, smooth tone said, "Don't worry, Kerry. I'll take care of it."

Kerry didn't ask how. Nor did she want to know.

After Simon hung up the phone, he called Commissioner Robertson and explained the situation he was facing with Nick Handley's confession and the presence of Alex Johnson in their lives, and offered a suggestion of what he thought should be done.

Twenty minutes after Simon had ended his call with Commissioner Robertson, Josh received an official transfer request.

Nick Handley was being transferred to Toronto where he would be facing charges for extortion and assault. Lake Pines would no longer be dealing with his case.

CHAPTER 59

Blue was the color that Lucia was most fond of, while Dominique was more interested in Sylvie's long silky hair. As Joyce worked at a table helping Lucia bead a small bracelet, Sylvie held Dominique captivated with a rolling melody as she sang softly in the corner of the room.

One of the pictures that captivated Kerry when she first came to Joyce's home had been painted by Sylvie. Its familiarity was difficult to place, and it wasn't until Kerry was introduced to Joyce's granddaughter that she realized that it was the same girl she watched paint under the pavilion at the art exhibit.

Kerry placed her hand gently on Joyce's arm, "What is that song that Sylvie is singing to Dominique?"

"It's a traditional Cree lullaby," Joyce said. "I sang it to all my children when they were young, now Sylvie is teaching the traditional songs to other people."

"What's it about?" Kerry asked.

"Every song is a story that is either meant to teach children a lesson or to tell them something about our past," Joyce explained. "The song that Sylvie is singing now is about a young cub that gets separated from his family when he becomes distracted while chasing a small butterfly. The mother bear calls out to her cub and the cub calls back, echoing her words. Eventually, they find each other and embrace."

Kerry smiled, knowing that the story is how Joyce would have wanted her search for Adam to turn out.

"Where is Sylvie teaching these songs?" Kerry asked.

"Online," Joyce smiled. "It took me a while to understand all of the technology, but once I watched her first class, I understood how many people she was able to reach. She's planning on releasing a recording of some of the songs this summer."

"That's a great idea," Kerry said. "I also saw her down at the waterfront during the art exhibit. She's very talented."

Pride filled Joyce's eyes, "Yes, she is. Her dream is to become an artist."

Kerry smiled and replied, “Joyce, she already is.”

CHAPTER 60

Kerry dropped Lucia off at home and she parked in her driveway, listening to Dominique's deep whistful breathing from the back seat of the car. She had fallen asleep within minutes of turning out of Joyce's driveway after an afternoon filled with excitement and play.

Since the night she was attacked, a sense of dread overcame Kerry every time she pulled into the driveway. She watched her daughter's reflection in the rearview mirror and knew that she had to do everything she could to protect her, and part of that had to be watching what she said to the media.

It wasn't the reporter's fault that he had printed what he did. After all, the taunting and insulting words came from Kerry's mouth. Even though it wasn't Dan who had been responsible for Dominique's attempted abduction or the attack in her driveway, Kerry knew she had to avoid drawing negative attention into their lives.

She had been thinking about making the call days earlier, but it wasn't until she asked Joyce's advice that she knew it was the right choice. As she sat in her driveway listening to the comforting sounds of Dominique sound asleep, she pulled out her phone and dialed Henry's number.

When Henry realized who was calling him, he was surprised and confused. Kerry received Joyce's approval before deciding to make the offer to Henry, but as she realized the excitement and eagerness in his voice she knew it was the right decision.

He was being invited to the official ribbon-cutting ceremony that was to take place at the site where a memorial would be built. In addition, Henry was being invited to share the children's stories through written accounts. The interviews would be in their family's words, and by their approval, and in exchange Henry would have exclusivity to their stories.

It was time, Kerry knew, to put aside the antagonistic approach she took with the reporters at the newspaper. Maybe together they could find a way to help the people of Lake Pines heal.

CHAPTER 61

Ada Denmark was seated next to Cleveland York when Simon walked into the room. Simon's request to meet with Cleveland York was met with less apprehension than he anticipated and within six hours of his call, Cleveland arrived at the station with his lawyer.

"Thank you for coming in," Simon said as he took a seat. "I assume your lawyer filled you in on what has happened since we last spoke?"

Ada reached out and grabbed Cleveland's hand, "I'm not here as a lawyer."

Simon raised his eyebrows, he hadn't seen that coming.

"She's my daughter," Cleveland clarified. He then placed his second hand over Ada's. "She's here for moral support."

"Do you want to have a lawyer present?" Simon asked.

"Am I being charged for a crime?" Cleveland asked.

Simon shook his head, "No."

Cleveland was the next to speak, "I feel like I owe you an explanation. I wasn't completely honest about the information I had."

"I gathered as much when your lawyer, or daughter, showed up at the property at East River Bridge."

"I was just trying to protect the family, but I can see now that it was the wrong decision. But before you jump to any conclusions of my guilt, I want to explain what exactly happened all those years ago."

Simon sat back in his chair.

"You are already aware of how my grandfather obtained the land in Lake Pines, it was the same in many small towns across the country. We had already sold much of the property, but for obvious reasons, we decided to hold onto the property in Lake Pines."

"So you did know about the bodies in the field?"

"Sort of. Around twenty years ago I decided to sell off several properties around the country that weren't being used. A photo of the land that you know as Belvedere Field caught my eye because of the spectacular view and I decided to keep it for myself. I thought it would be an ideal location to build a cottage and I sent out a foreman from one of my divisions to survey the land."

"That's when you found the body," Simon thought back to Gavin's comment about one of the bodies being disturbed and then reburied.

Cleveland nodded. "I instructed the crew to cover as much of their work in the field as they could and to return home. At the time, my father was still running York Enterprises, and I confronted him about what was found in the field. Reluctantly he told me what had transpired. My father was politically connected, and even more aggressive than my grandfather was in business. A small upstart pharmaceutical company had approached my father with a proposal for a trial drug, but they needed government approval and money before they could begin the tests."

"And your father had access to both of those things."

"Through my father's connections, they received the government approval to run the test facility, although it was agreed by both parties that the project was to remain confidential. York Enterprises would be the company to manufacture and distribute the drug, should the trials be successful, and the government would receive preferential supply for their own patients. He had called it a win-win situation."

"But it wasn't, Mr. York," Simon said. "Kids were taken without their family's knowledge and used in the trial. All of those kids died."

Cleveland nodded, "I know. But I had no way of knowing the identity of those bodies, or any of the other patients for that matter. My father said the files were destroyed and that the medical facility was disbanded when the doctor in charge of the facility was killed by one of the patients. The trial ended before they had a chance to complete the treatment for the experimental drug. The surviving patients were transferred to different hospitals around the province and the ones who had died and were buried on the property had been moved so they couldn't be connected to York Enterprises."

"You are aware that charges are going to be brought against York Enterprises for their involvement in the facility, as well as the continued concealment of the bodies in the field?"

"I do," Cleveland said. "And we'll fight them. But only to a point."

"What do you mean?"

"The role my father played in the establishment of the medical facility, as well as the transfer of the bodies, was wrong. I won't argue with you on that. But I can't let York Enterprises take all the blame when there were so many other parties involved."

Simon knew that Cleveland had the power and money to fight the charges in court, and although he was correct to point out the guilt of other parties involved, it wasn't going to change Simon's mind.

Ada released her father's hand, reached into her bag, and pulled out an envelope.

"Now, I am here as a lawyer," she slid the envelope across Simon's desk. "This is a proposed agreement. In it, there's a sizeable donation for a memorial, funding for the establishment for an independent tribunal, and the ownership of two parcels of land will be transferred to the town of Lake Pines."

"Is this in exchange for us not charging you with a crime?" Simon asked.

Cleveland York stood, buttoned his jacket closed, and smiled, "No. What's being offered in that envelope is effective immediately and regardless of your actions toward me or my company. I will fight whatever charges you come forward with, but the victims and their families deserve to be acknowledged."

"But why now? Why this?" Simon said, holding up the envelope.

"There are always casualties, Officer, the trick is to not be one of them."

Ada slipped her hand around her father's arm, they turned around and walked out the door.

CHAPTER 62

Finding the truth of who owned Belvedere Field and the concern that another accusation would threaten Thomas' career, forced him to be honest and open to everyone around him. It also helped him mend an awkward relationship with their neighbor.

Since the day that Thomas enlisted Bill Gibbon's help, he had found his neighbor less antagonistic. He even waved when Thomas was mowing the lawn as opposed to complaining about the noise. Bill no longer measured the distance between the garbage can and the curb, nor did he complain about small twigs that had blown onto his lawn.

In addition to mending the proverbial fence with his neighbor, Thomas wanted to ensure that their home and his worksite had the highest grade security system installed. Never again would he be caught off guard or put the lives of those he cared about in harm's way.

His connections in the construction industry gave him access to top-of-the-line security cameras, high-grade lighting, and impenetrable locks. All of which he had purchased. Alex Johnson was still on the loose, and the threat he posed to both Dominique, Kerry, and Josh was enough to convince everyone to upgrade their security.

Thomas had spent the morning with Oliver installing new lighting, locks, and a security system that recorded all movement around the house onto a closed system computer at Kerry and Simon's home. The afternoon hours would be spent installing the same equipment at his home.

Oliver was handing Thomas the metal cover for the light fixture above the back door when Bill walked into the yard.

"I see you're putting up some new lights," Bill said as he looked at the row of wires leading to the new fixture.

Thomas dropped his arms to his side, and leaned on the top of the ladder looking down at Bill, "I hope you're not going to tell me I need a special permit for this equipment."

Bill let a small smile trickle across his face, which was an unfamiliar response from his neighbor.

"No, I just wanted to see if you needed any help."

The suggestion took Thomas by surprise. He looked around the yard and nodded toward the back fence, "I could use some help installing the new lock on the gate."

Without another word, Bill grabbed a couple of tools and the new lock as he headed to the far end of the yard. Thomas climbed down from the ladder once he secured the final piece of the light to the side of the house, and joined Bill who was measuring the width of the gate.

Bill pointed to a spot on the fence post, "You know, if you put the lock at this height then it'll be more difficult for kids to get it open."

"Great idea," Thomas placed a mark on the board with a pencil and then lined up the metal for the lock.

It took a few tries to line up the sliding bolt, but soon they were finished and packing their tools in the shed.

"You know Bill, I really appreciated your help."

"No problem. I've spent hours tinkering around the house, putting a bolt onto a gate is no big deal."

"I mean when you helped me find the owners of Belvedere Field."

"Oh, that," Bill said.

"I was thinking," Thomas began. "Now that things have settled down and I have the construction site up and running again, I'm going to need some help ensuring we have all the right certifications."

"I can recommend a couple of guys that could help you out," Bill said. "I'll drop off their name and numbers for you and you can give them a call."

Thomas shook his head, "No. I was hoping you'd consider joining my team."

Bill's mouth dropped open, "Me?"

"Yeah," Thomas laughed. "Why are you so surprised?"

"I don't know. I guess since I've been away from working in the department for so long, I'm surprised you wouldn't want someone more up to speed on regulations and by-laws."

"You have two things that I need. Resourcefulness and trust," Thomas held his hand out. "What do you say?"

Bill grabbed Thomas' hand, "You've got yourself a deal."

CHAPTER 63

In the end, it was Thomas' idea to construct a memorial on Belvedere Field. The land was officially donated by York Enterprises, and the monument would be privately funded by Cleveland York. It was unanimously agreed that the field would be renamed, but neither a name nor a vision for the monument had been established yet.

Thinking back to the artists under the pavilion at the art exhibit, Kerry suggested that the youth in Lake Pines be asked to contribute art to the design. Thomas worked with the families, offering his crew's time and expertise to design and build the monument on the field. Although the exact design hadn't been confirmed, everyone wanted to build a place where people could meet and heal. It would be a place to honor the lives lost, but it would also be a place where they could be remembered.

Joyce arrived at the field an hour before the ribbon-cutting ceremony, and she invited Kerry to join her. She wanted to thank Kerry privately for her work and tenacity in giving each of the unknown victims a name and reuniting their spirit with their families.

"I have a feeling that you're not a person who takes no for an answer," Joyce smiled.

"If you only knew," Kerry replied with a wink. "What are you going to do now?"

“I want to help other families heal, whether we’re able to locate their children or not. I think a lot of that will start with education. Sylvie is helping me set up an online platform so I can connect with communities across the country.”

“You know that’ll mean you need to figure out that ‘techy’ stuff you were making fun of.” Kerry joked.

“I know!” Joyce looped her arm around Kerry’s and they walked a little further before she handed her a bracelet, “These are Adam’s favorite colors. I wanted you to have it.”

Kerry lay the beaded bracelet on her wrist and Joyce tied the band, securing it to her arm. The two women held a long embrace, as mothers and as new friends. Joyce smiled and thanked Kerry one more time before she turned around and walked toward the frame of what was to be the lasting memorial.

In the years that passed since the day Adam went missing, Joyce's body settled into sadness and began to shrink. Her mouth, which captured a smile in youthful pictures, had fought the urge to smile, feeling the sting every time she remembered her son. But slowly the peace would return.

The afternoon Kerry arrived at Joyce's home with the news of finding Adam's body, Joyce allowed herself one final burst to grieve. Her mouth bent forward and the lids of her eyes sloped down, and tears came in torrents. Her skin, speckled with the ravages of time displayed a sallowness as she mourned. Joyce seemed unable to remember the shape of a smile, or the natural happiness in her eyes that, once, came so effortlessly.

The moments it did show, it was because Joyce Thibert forced it.

But today, she seemed more at ease.

Although the happiness would never completely return, a purpose and a focus had entered her life and it was to ensure remembrance for the children who were gone.

When the hidden graves were unearthed, thousands of voices unheard years earlier, rose into the air. Cries for justice were released by the songs of remembrance being sung by the people who gathered for the ribbon-cutting ceremony. On the same field where innocent victims were so unceremoniously concealed, healing could start to begin.

It would take time. A long time.

And it would take honest participation from everyone involved. It would be the legacy left for future generations if they could only find the strength to admit what was wrong - and to do what is right. The children's deaths would be silent deaths that would remain silent no more, at least by those willing to hear the cries.

Sturdily taking each step, forcing confidence and strength where there had lived pain and sorrow for so many years, Joyce made her way down the hill. Kerry watched as her body grew smaller the farther she walked and she was filled with an overwhelming sense of sadness. She had helped Joyce find answers to the questions she carried for so long but in doing so left her with so many more unanswered.

The monument would stand in honor of the young victims found in Belvedere Field, and as a reminder for many more who were still missing. Evil permanently shifts everyone around it, whether they are the intended target or not. The proof is in the lives left behind.

Kerry let out a deep breath and waited for what she thought was an appropriate amount of time before she turned around to join the others who were waiting by the edge of the road.

The End

"Don't let the echoes of guilt be the excuse for eluding our responsibility to the past. Accountability does not end because our footprints have faded. Instead, our presence is demanded because of the fear that the memories will drift into obscurity, and we must fight to keep each and every one of them alive."

Did you enjoy this book? You can make a difference.

Reviews are the most powerful tools in my arsenal when it comes to getting attention for my books. And I have something more powerful than a New York Publisher. I have you – my reader.

If you've enjoyed this book, I would be very grateful if you could just spend five minutes leaving a review (it can be as short as you like) and it will help bring my books to the attention of other readers.

Thank you very much.

About the Author

L.L. Abbott is the author of the popular Lake Pines Mystery Series, The Anna Ledin Spy Thriller Series, and many standalone novels, spanning several genres. She makes her online home at www.llabbott.com, where you can find links to all her books.

Free Books, Downloads and Contests

Go to www.llabbott.com/Contact to join our reading community.

Made in the USA
Middletown, DE
20 September 2024

61169230R10350